THE
BEAUTIFUL
Ones

THE BEAUTIFUL
Ones

ESSENCE BESTSELLING AUTHOR
ADRIANNE BYRD

ARABESQUE®

Recycling programs
for this product may
not exist in your area.

THE BEAUTIFUL ONES

ISBN-13: 978-0-373-53480-7

First published by BET Publications, LLC in 2005

Copyright © 2012 by Adrianne Byrd

www.kimanipress.com

Printed in U.S.A.

Dear Reader,

I hope you enjoy the rerelease of *The Beautiful Ones,* the third book in a series that introduces best friends Ophelia Missler and Solomon Bassett. This story also includes one of the heartbreaking Hinton brothers. Although the books were never meant to become a series, I fell in love with the characters and so have the fans. And voilà, the series continues to this day, and includes the House of Kings trilogy, which features the Hintons' cousins: Eamon, Xavier and Jeremy King.

I hope you like this story about how friends become lovers, and how true love is sometimes closer than you think. In this case, when push comes to shove, Ophelia and Solomon discover that their feelings are more than just platonic.

In addition to *The Beautiful Ones,* look for the rest of the books in the series: *Unforgettable* and *Comfort of a Man,* as well as *Feel the Fire* and *Love Takes Time,* which are already available. Next month readers will finally get to read the much-anticipated love story of Quentin Hinton. Stay tuned and visit me on my website, www.adriannebyrd.com, and sign up for the newsletter so that you can be informed of all my latest releases.

Until then, I wish you the best of love,

Adrianne Byrd

To Kathy Alba:
Best friends for life

Prologue

Flight 1269 for Los Angeles was delayed. Toni Wright entered through the lobby doors of the cocktail lounge of the airline's Crown Room in desperate need of a drink. Instead her eyes zeroed in on a handsome brother at the bar who looked like he wanted to drown his sorrows in his glass.

Fleetingly, she wondered what could be so bad, but the last thing she wanted to do was play Dear Abby to some stranger. She stopped at the bar and ordered a Cosmopolitan. As she waited, her gaze drifted back to the stranger.

He was tall, just like she liked them, and well dressed. In fact, his aura seemed to drip with power and prestige—which definitely wasn't a negative.

She wished he would look up so she could see his eyes. She had a feeling they were beautiful.

"Here you go, ma'am," the bartender said.

Toni smiled and laid down a tip. She turned to walk away but then felt compelled to make small talk with the brooding brother. Why not? Her best friend, Brooklyn, had met the love of her life in a bar—maybe lightning would strike twice.

"A penny for your thoughts," she said, and then cringed at the campy line. When he didn't respond, she felt like an idiot. Never one to shy away from a challenge, Toni settled into the chair next to him.

It was a good thing, too; the man's heavenly fragrance was seductive enough to melt off a woman's panties.

He reached for his glass and drained the rest of his drink.

"Buy you another?" she asked.

Finally, he glanced her way. Just as she thought—he had beautiful eyes.

"I always thought men were supposed to do the asking, not the other way around?"

Toni's toes curled at the velvety smoothness of his voice. "I figured we could make an exception, seeing how you look as if you need it."

A corner of his lips curled and an adorable dimple appeared. "That's very kind of you, but—"

"And if it makes you feel better, you can buy my next one." She winked and flashed him her best smile.

He hesitated, looked her over, and then nodded. "Deal."

While Toni signaled for the bartender, she could feel the man's eyes linger on her. She hoped he liked what he saw, but there were no guarantees, since she'd dressed down for travel.

"You're a lawyer," he said flatly.

Astonished, she glanced back at him. "How did you know that?"

He smiled again. "You have that look about you."

"Oh?" She crossed her arms. "And what look is that?"

"The I-can-eat-anyone-alive-and-still-have-room-for-dessert look."

She laughed and managed to maintain eye contact. "Does that look scare you?"

"Very little scares me." His smile diminished, but he remained polite.

"Another scotch on the rocks for the gentleman," the bartender announced.

For a few minutes after the drink was delivered, Toni found herself at a loss as to how to keep the conversation going. She had already used the penny-for-your-thoughts line, and she just wasn't willing to demean herself by asking for his zodiac sign.

"Thanks for the drink, but I don't think I'm going to be very good company," he said.

She considered him for a moment and warred with herself as to whether to stay or leave. "You know, I've been told I'm a pretty good listener," she said. "And it looks like I have plenty of time to kill."

"You don't want to hear my sob story."

"Oh, I don't know." She smiled. "Maybe I can help."

"Trust me. I've heard it all. Trouble don't last always. This, too, shall pass. Or my personal favorite—there are plenty of fish in the sea."

Genuine concern crept into her voice. "So, someone broke your heart?"

"That's putting it mildly."

Toni drew a deep breath. "Who was she?"

"Someone...very special," he whispered. "Someone I loved the moment I laid eyes on her."

She waited for him to continue, but she saw she had to nudge a little more. "Does this someone have a name?"

He nodded. "Yes—Ophelia Missler. I guess you could say it all started at a wedding..."

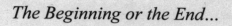

The Beginning or the End...

Chapter 1

On a beautiful June day, Marcel Taylor and Diana Guy spoke their vows before God, friends, and family. It was a nontraditional wedding where Brandy—Marcel's ninety-pound Doberman pinscher—served as the ring bearer. Timothy Banks, Diana's best friend and neighbor, stood as the maid of honor—in a tux, and Ophelia Missler, one of Marcel's closest childhood friends, took her place as a groomsman.

After the priest introduced Mr. and Mrs. Marcel Taylor to the guests, a shower of rose petals descended on the smiling couple.

Louisa Mae Styles, Diana's grandmother and a cancer survivor, couldn't stop crying, and now demanded that the couple get busy producing babies.

Donald and Camille Taylor, Marcel's parents, said their congratulations to the couple and also hassled them about grandchildren.

At the reception, Solomon Bassett, Marcel's best friend and business partner, approached Ophelia for a dance.

As he took her into his arms, he marveled at how long he, Ophelia, and Marcel had been the best of friends.

Solomon first met Marcel when his family moved next door to the Bassetts in the summer of '78. Their love of sports was all it took to seal their life-long friendship. It was the year when Reggie Jackson, O.J. Simpson, Muhammad Ali, and Kareem Abdul-Jabbar ruled their world. Solomon and Marcel vowed to be the first athletes to win the Super Bowl, the NBA finals, and the World Series. Life was good.

In the winter of '81, Ophelia, a scrawny girl who they originally suspected had cooties, wormed her way into their private club. It was hard to ignore her. She could sail a fastball past the best players in the neighborhood and could run like the wind. Life was better.

By the time puberty hit, Ophelia's long, thin legs suddenly had shape to them, and her round bottom was a nice distraction in Gloria Vanderbilt jeans. And Lord, her breasts. Solomon, to this day, didn't know where they came from, but suddenly she had them, and they were the best pair in their junior high school. His brotherly affection toward her had changed overnight, and life had never been the same.

Ophelia was amazingly beautiful, with her perfect honey-coated skin and mesmerizing topaz-colored eyes. Today her thick, sandy brown hair with streaks of blond was pressed iron straight and hung like a beautiful curtain to the center of her back.

Solomon had never found the words to tell Ophelia about his feelings, mainly because she always had seemed more attracted to Marcel. But, in a recent talk at one of their favorite cafés, Solomon had relayed the story of how Marcel was snared by his former secretary, Diana, and Ophelia had revealed that she'd once harbored a secret crush on him.

Maybe things were finally about to change between them.

He wasn't too happy that she had brought a date to the wedding, but hey, it wasn't like he had any right to be jealous.

"I'm glad you told me about their love story," Ophelia said, beaming at the couple. "They look so happy."

"I have a feeling that they are." He drew in a deep breath. "Ophelia, there's something I've been dying to tell you."

"There's something I have to tell you, too," she said, smiling.

"Oh?"

"Yeah, I told Jonas about Marcel and Diana—"

"Who?"

"My date—Jonas Hinton." She frowned. "You never pay attention to me, do you?"

"Of course I do." He tried to cover up with a smile.

"Well, anyway, Jonas and I have been dating for a while, and last night he popped the question."

Solomon's heart dropped. "What question?"

Ophelia slapped him on the shoulder. "*The* question, silly. Now, we haven't picked out a ring, but…we're getting married." She bounced excitedly against him. "Isn't that great?"

He stopped dancing. "What?"

Her smile started to ebb away. "Aren't you happy for me?"

Slowly he managed a butterfly smile. "That's great."

"I know it's a shock." She giggled. "But don't tell

Marcel and Diana. I don't want to take anything away from their day."

"My lips are sealed."

She leaned in and kissed his cheek. "Thanks. You know I want you and Marcel to serve as bridesmaids."

He managed a chuckle. "I wouldn't miss that for the world."

He managed to finish the dance with some semblance of dignity, but soon found himself at the bar.

"What's with the long face?" Marcel asked, slapping him on the back as he joined him. "No one should be frowning at my wedding."

"Don't worry about me, man. I'm fine. Congratulations again." He looked around. "Where's Diana?"

"Upstairs changing. It's about time we leave you guys for our honeymoon in Bermuda."

"Ah, white sands and pastel-colored buildings."

"Paradise for thirty days."

"I'm jealous."

"Shouldn't be." He draped an arm around Solomon's shoulder. "I see Ophelia showed up with Jonas."

"Yeah. Don't remind me."

"You know, you better get in there before he snatches up your girl. A woman can only wait for so long."

"You've been married an hour, and already you've turned into Dear Abby."

Marcel held up his hands. "Just trying to help."

Solomon bobbed his head and glanced back at the dance floor to see Ophelia floating in Jonas's arms.

Minutes later, Diana appeared at the top of the stairs dressed in an all-white linen suit. Below her, a small crowd of single women gathered around for the tossing of the bridal bouquet.

The crowd gasped when an unladylike shove awarded

Nora Gibson, a wickedly ambitious employee at T & B Entertainment, the prize instead of Marcel's thirteen-year-old cousin.

"I got it. I got it."

"You sure did, honey." Willy Bassett, Solomon's philandering uncle, beamed at her as she slid next to him.

"Now that's a crazy match," Marcel whispered to Diana.

Seconds later, Solomon won the garter-belt toss. He gave Ophelia a long, meaningful glance and then held the garter up for a loud cheer from the crowd.

More rose petals rained down on Marcel and Diana as they made their mad dash to their limo. While Solomon was incredibly happy for the couple, who were embarking on a new chapter in their lives, he battled a tsunami of depression.

"Solomon?"

He turned toward the sweet sound of Ophelia's voice and ignored the tightening in his chest when he faced her.

"It looks like it's one down and two to go." Her full lips slid into a smile.

He hesitated before finally replying. "Not for long."

Her cheeks flushed prettily before a tall, light-skinned brother slid next to her and draped an arm around her waist.

"Hey, baby. I brought you a drink," the man said, and then cast a curious glance at Solomon. "Hello, I'm Jonas." He jutted out a hand.

Solomon straightened and sized up Ophelia's fiancé. Both men stood at an even six-two, but where Solomon looked the part of a clean-cut, scholarly type, Jonas looked as though he were born to be on a Hollywood screen. In fact, Solomon couldn't remember ever seeing a man with such long, curly lashes.

Ophelia coughed, and Solomon suddenly realized that he hadn't responded to the man's introduction.

"Solomon," he said, accepting Jonas's hand. The men pumped each other's arms with more strength than was necessary.

"It's nice to finally meet you," Jonas said, but there was very little warmth in his eyes. "Ophelia talks a lot about you."

Solomon's gaze returned to hers. "Is that right?"

"Yeah," Jonas continued. "If I didn't know any better, I'd think I'd have to watch her around you."

Ophelia playfully slapped Jonas on the chest. "Solomon and I are just friends."

Just friends. Solomon forced a smile. "Well, let me be the first to wish you the best of luck. Any ideas when this happy event will take place?"

Ophelia rolled her eyes heavenward. "Well—"

"The sooner the better," Jonas answered. "I know I'm hoping for something before the new year."

Solomon's heart dropped.

"That's just around the corner," Ophelia said, astonished.

"What can I say? I can't wait to make you a Hinton." He leaned down and gave her a quick peck on the nose.

"And I can't wait to be a Hinton," she responded, gazing up at him.

"All this gushy sweet stuff is bad for my diabetes," Solomon said with a healthy dose of sarcasm. "If you two will excuse me." He turned and walked away.

He hadn't moved more than a few feet when he felt a restraining hand against his shoulder. Turning, he once again faced Ophelia—minus the fiancé.

"Hey, what's the matter?" she asked, frowning. "Aren't you happy for me?"

He didn't want to answer that. "Of course I am."

Her brows rose as if she detected his lie.

"I'm just shocked," he amended. "I didn't even know that you were seeing someone seriously. You never mentioned it."

Her smile trembled a bit while she shrugged. "Well, I guess it happened kind of fast."

He studied her for a moment before he cast a glance over her shoulder to see Jonas watching them from a distance. "Just how long have you been seeing this guy?"

She shrugged again. "Not long…maybe four months."

"Four months?" he echoed. "You hardly know him."

"That's not true," she said defensively.

"What's his mother's maiden name?"

She blinked. "I don't know. What does that have to do with anything?"

"What's my mother's maiden name?"

"Baker."

He smiled and crossed his arms. "How does he like his coffee?"

"He, uh…"

"How do I like my coffee?"

Ophelia hesitated.

"Well?"

"Milk, no cream, no sugar."

"I think I made my point."

"But I love him," she admitted, settling her hands on her hips.

Her words wiped the smug smile from Solomon's lips and plunged the blade of jealousy deeper into his heart. "Then I wish you all the happiness in the world."

Ophelia's face lit up as she leaned up on her toes

and brushed a kiss against his cheek. "Thanks, Solomon. You have no idea what it means to me to hear you say that."

"Ophelia?" Jonas's voice floated over to them.

"You better go," Solomon said. "I think your fiancé is getting nervous."

"A little jealousy won't hurt him." She winked, kissed Solomon, and turned away.

Solomon watched as she returned to her fiancé's side. For a brief moment, his gaze met Jonas's, and he felt as if the man could read his mind. Exhaling a long breath, Solomon turned away and went in search of the open bar. "I need a drink."

Chapter 2

Jonas looped his arm possessively around Ophelia's small waist. "I'd say that your *friend* doesn't seem too happy with our news."

"Who—Solomon?" Ophelia frowned as she accepted another piece of the teardrop coconut cake. "He's just surprised. Probably starting to feel left out since I'm following in Marcel's footsteps."

"Nah." Jonas's gaze cut away from Solomon's lone form at the bar to settle on her. "That's not it."

"Sure it is." She sank her fork into the dessert, and then moaned in ecstasy as she took her first bite. "This cake is the bomb," she muttered, and quickly shoved another forkful into her mouth.

Jonas laughed and shook his head. "I'm glad you're enjoying it."

"You don't understand, baby. Here, try some." She prepared a bite for him and lifted it for him to sample.

He opened his mouth obligingly and then mimicked her exaggerated, orgasmic moans, complete with dramatic eye rolls.

"Oh, quit it." Ophelia smacked his arm. "You're not funny."

Chuckling, he pulled her close. "What? I love it when you make those sounds," he whispered into her ear. "I'm looking forward to hearing them for the rest of our lives."

She giggled and glanced around to see whether they were being watched. Her body stiffened when her gaze caught Solomon's from across the pavilion.

He lifted his glass in a silent salute and then turned away.

"You still want to tell me that there's nothing between you two?" Jonas's voice sharpened with sarcasm.

Ophelia ignored the sudden queasy tightness in her stomach and shrugged indifferently. "It's not what you think." She pulled out of his arms.

"And what exactly am I thinking?"

Ophelia drew an impatient breath, but somehow managed to hold on to her smile. "Can we just drop the subject? Once you get to know Solomon, you two are going to be as thick as thieves."

Jonas's expression radiated doubt.

"C'mon." She set aside her half-eaten cake and reached for his hands. "Dance with me."

"Who me?" he asked, as she led him back across the pavilion and over to the dance floor. "I can't dance, remember?"

"Sure you can," she insisted and navigated them to the center of the floor.

"Ophelia, I don't know about this."

She faced him with another wide smile and showed

him how to properly position his hands. "Now just follow my lead," she coached.

"I have a feeling that's not going to be the last time I hear those words," he joked, and then concentrated perhaps a little too much on his dance movements.

"Relax." She slinked and wiggled against him. "Just feel the music. Let your body go."

Jonas followed her instruction, but still managed to look as stiff as a board, so much so that Ophelia had a hard time suppressing her amusement.

"Okay. All right. Enough." A lazy grin hugged his lips as he grabbed her wrist and led her off the dance floor. "I'd like to reserve making an ass out of myself to private parties only. If you don't mind."

Ophelia's head rocked back with a hearty bark of laughter. "But you were so cute," she whined playfully.

Jonas slowed down when they reached the lawn, which was still jammed tight with people. He gave a cursory glance around and drew her back into his arms. "So, are you ready to blow this taco stand so we can do a little celebrating ourselves?"

"Oh?" She lifted her head in keen interest. "What exactly do you have in mind?"

Glancing up at the clear blue sky, Jonas mulled the question over. "I'm thinking about a candlelight dinner for two."

"Italian?" she suggested her favorite.

"Of course. We can put on some music—"

"But there's no dancing."

He shrugged. "I don't know. I might be able to manage a little cheek-to-cheek action. But then afterward—"

"Ah, ah, ah, lover boy." She waved her finger at him. "There will be none of that." At Jonas's confused look, she added, "We're engaged."

"I'm following you so far."

Ophelia's body warmed deliciously as she playfully walked her fingers up the center of his chest. "Well, I was thinking, since we're going to have such a short engagement that maybe it's best that we...abstain until our wedding night."

Jonas's body stiffened, and his eyes widened in stunned disbelief. "Come again?"

Ophelia couldn't help but smile at his reaction. "Don't you want our wedding night to be special?"

"It's already going to be special." He hugged her tighter. "It will be the first time we'll make love as man and wife."

"You know what I mean." She lowered her voice. "I mean in the traditional sense. No sex before marriage."

"If that's the case, we're already S.O.L.," he said, leaning toward her and stealing a kiss. "I'm already familiar with every inch of you."

"Good," she cooed. "Then you won't have any problems hanging on to those memories until our wedding night."

Their eyes met.

"You're serious, aren't you?" Jonas's voice ended on a note of horror.

"Dead serious. Our waiting is supposed to heighten the anticipation. I'm up for the challenge." With a teasing smile and a flirtatious wink, Ophelia slowly eased out of his arms and sashayed away from him. It was a game she loved to play with him. In her head, she timed how long it would take for him to follow her. This time, she counted to three—a new record.

"Okay," Jonas said. "Let's say that I do agree to this crazy idea."

She faced him with a syrupy smile.

"And I'm not saying that I am," he clarified. "But if I did, what exactly *can* we do until our wedding night?"

Once again, Ophelia slid her arms up his chest and locked them around his neck. "We can still kiss and cuddle."

"What am I—in kindergarten?"

"Kindergarten?" She laughed. "I didn't receive my first kiss until I was in junior high—and that didn't really count."

Jonas frowned. "Why?"

Ophelia shrugged and rolled her eyes. "Because it was just Solomon."

"I wish those two would just go get a room," Solomon said in disgust. He tossed back his fourth shot and then growled through the burn. "Hit me again," he commanded the bartender.

"Are you all right, sir?" The lanky man reached for Solomon's poison of choice and splashed out another shot.

"Peachy," Solomon answered, and then downed the drink in the same breath.

"There's my favorite nephew," Willy's voice thundered a half a second before his heavy hand swatted across Solomon's back. "I wondered where you took off to."

"Well, you found me."

"Boy, I tell you that Marcel really knows how to throw a shindig. Of course, if it were my party, I would have thrown in a few strippers."

"It's a wedding, Uncle Willy."

"Yeah, so?"

Solomon shook his head and then barked at the bartender again, "Hit me."

"Whatcha doin'?" Willy asked.

"Getting drunk."

"Sounds like fun. Mind if I play?"

"It's a free country."

"Not to mention an open bar." Willy laughed and settled his large frame on a stool next to Solomon before he signaled the bartender. I'll have what he's having." When he received his drink, he held it up. "Should we at least toast to something?"

"Sure, why not?" He lifted his glass. "How about to…no more women?"

Willy pulled his glass away. "Good Lord, I can't toast to that. I adore women. Of course, I can't say that they're always overly fond of me… But I always seem to find another fish in the ocean, if you catch my drift."

Solomon grunted and rolled his eyes. "Well, you can have them." He set his drink back down on the bar, uncertain whether he would be able to handle another shot without tipping off his stool.

Willy's boisterous laugh rang out and drew attention from people across the pavilion. "What's with this crazy talk?" He swung his meaty arm around Solomon's shoulders. "There's more than enough fish for the two of us, especially now that Casanova Brown has hung up his shoes. Hell, I'm practically salivating at the possibilities. You saw the little saucy number I came here with, didn't you?"

"Nora Gibson?" Solomon laughed. "Let me give *you* some advice, old man. Run. Run like hell and don't look back."

"Ah, hell, Solomon. There's nothing wrong with a lady who has a little spice…or a dangerous edge. It keeps things interesting. You remember Glenda?"

Solomon rolled his eyes. "How could I ever forget? She put you in the hospital for what, six weeks?"

Willy nodded. "Uh-huh. Good woman—salt of the earth."

"She's doing five to ten for stabbing you."

"Hey, I was to blame for some of that. I should've never gotten caught nailing her sister in Glenda's bed. Of course, who knows, Glenda and I might get back together when she gets out. The things that woman can do with her mouth...."

Solomon frowned. "Didn't you marry Glenda's sister?"

Willy sighed dreamily. "Yeah. It was the best sixty-two hours of my life. But then there was a third sister—"

"Stop. Please stop," Solomon begged, and then tossed back his last shot. "None of this is convincing me not to give up women."

"What's the alternative?" Willy lowered his voice to a normal level. "You're not trying to tell me you're a little...funny, are you?" He quickly held up his arms. "Not that I'm saying there is anything wrong with that. It's just that I would have never thought—"

"Relax. I'm not gay."

Willy's shoulders slumped with obvious relief. "Well, then. What are we talking about? You can't just give up sex—you'll explode. Trust me, I know. One time..."

Solomon slumped his head against the palm of his hand and tuned out another one of his uncle's wild sex-capades. Right now, Solomon just wanted the alcohol to kick in and numb the sharp pain of his broken heart. The problem was, he had no one to blame but himself.

He couldn't count the number of times Marcel had urged him to come clean with Ophelia—nor could he remember how many times he'd practiced doing just that in front of the bathroom mirror. But in Solomon's heart, he knew such a confession could ruin their friendship. And he never wanted that.

He also didn't want to watch her marry someone else.

"—So I guess my point, nephew, is that the best way to get over a woman is to find another woman." Willy pounded Solomon's back. "It's a hell of a better solution than giving them up."

Solomon nodded and glanced across the lawn again to see Ophelia and her fiancé climb into a limo. "You know, Uncle Willy, I just might take your advice this time around."

Chapter 3

"Alone at last," Jonas whispered from behind Ophelia as they stood in one of his spacious bachelor pads in the heart of downtown Atlanta.

Ophelia stood still while her fiancé took his time lowering the zipper on the back of her blush-colored dress. She smiled at the sound of his soft intake of breath, and then trembled at the feel of his lips pressed against her shoulder blade. This was undoubtedly a test of his restraint, and Ophelia loved every minute of it.

It was true that in her younger years she was a tomboy, but by the time she finished college, Ophelia had mastered the art of seduction. Men were reduced to mere idiots in front of a pretty face and a curvy body.

However, her charms rarely worked on one man: Solomon Bassett. Who knows, maybe that was why she had such a crush on him for as long as she did. He was a challenge—and what woman didn't like a challenge?

Jonas kissed her other shoulder. "I don't know if I'm going to make it until our wedding night," he whispered. "It's only been a couple of hours, and I already feel like I'm going crazy."

Ophelia pushed all thoughts of Solomon to the back of her mind. "Has anyone ever told you that you have a way with words?" She faced him and winked. "I'm jumping in the shower."

Jonas groaned and pulled her closer before she could step away. "Are you sure that I can't talk you out of this nonsense? I mean, it *is* the twenty-first century."

Ophelia smiled and shook her head. "C'mon, baby. You're not even trying. If we do settle on a winter wedding, we're only talking about a few months."

"If?" He laughed. "Seven months it is. Any longer than that, and we'll just have to live the rest of our lives in sin and not get married."

"Then it's settled. January it is."

Jonas's adorable dimples flashed while his head lowered for a kiss. "You know I've always been partial to November."

"Five months? That's hardly enough time to—"

Jonas pressed his finger against her lips. "It's plenty of time. We'll hire the best damn wedding planner money can buy."

"Don't forget my mother…aunts…and cousins."

"See? We have plenty of help." His confident smile widened. "We'll have the most beautiful wedding the state of South Carolina has ever seen."

"South Carolina? We're getting married there?"

"Of course we are." He frowned and laughed at the same time. "My family is there."

Ophelia stepped back. "I know, but my family lives here in Atlanta."

He shrugged. "I'll buy them airline tickets."

"We can't just buy everyone airline tickets," she protested.

"Why not? I can afford it." He chuckled and pulled her back into his arms. "Or did you forget you were marrying a very wealthy man?"

"Just because you have money doesn't meant you have to be so frivolous with—"

"Frivolous?" he barked. His eyes danced with amusement. "We're talking about our wedding—not about some luxury toy we don't need."

"But flying my whole family—"

"Fine. We'll have the wedding here in Atlanta, and my family will fly down. Problem solved."

He leaned in for a kiss, but she quickly pushed him back. "How is that solving the problem? Your family is larger than mine. That's even more money."

"Hardly," he laughed. "My family can afford their own tickets."

"And what—my family can't?"

Jonas's expression twisted in confusion as his arms dropped to his sides. "Did I miss something?"

Ophelia stared at him, unsure where her sudden wave of irritation came from.

"Are you purposely trying to start an argument?" Jonas laughed.

Closing her eyes, Ophelia expelled a tired breath. "Forgive me. See? The wedding is already stressing me out."

He gently drew her back into his arms. "Well, I know a few things that can relax you."

One flash of his dimpled cheeks, and Ophelia was putty in his hands. "Are we back to that again?"

"I have a feeling that this is going to be a hot topic

for the next few months." His hands cupped and then lightly stroked her chin. "But if waiting is something you truly want to do, then we'll do it."

He smiled again and she watched as his head descended. Closing her eyes, she waited patiently for their lips to connect. This time there would be sparks—that magical something to reinforce her belief that this man was her destiny.

At last his soft lips pressed against hers and, just like the times before, her heart dropped in disappointment. It wasn't a bad kiss—far from it. However, she didn't get that warm tingling rush like when…

She abruptly pulled away from him. "I better jump in the shower."

When his expression twisted, she eased the situation with another smile. "You promised me Italian, remember?"

He studied her a second longer before bobbing his head. "Yeah. I'll speak with the chef." Jonas backed away and shoved his hands into his pants pockets. "Take your time."

Ophelia nodded and then sashayed her way toward the bathroom, knowing full well Jonas's gaze followed her every move. Once she closed the door, she quickly moved over to the shower.

What the hell was wrong with her? Jonas was an ideal catch. Any woman would be happy to have him. Not only was he good looking and successful, he was kind, caring, and attentive. What was there not to love?

She laughed at herself. She was being silly. Of course she loved Jonas. That whole speech Solomon gave about not knowing Jonas was just his way of playing the role of protector. That was what he'd always been to her, really—him and Marcel.

Casanova Brown married. She shook her head. She would've definitely put her money on him being the last—not the first in their screwball group to walk down the aisle. After all too many women, so little time had always been his motto.

Well, she was going to be next. Instant warmth radiated through her at the sweet memory of the day she'd met Jonas—"the asshole" as she and her business partner, Stevie, had affectionately christened him. As owners of Missler & Lambert Sports Rehabilitation Center, she and Stevie had actually worked for the Carolina Panthers for years. However, when the NFL team got a new owner, Ophelia and Stevie received a pink slip almost immediately. Having never been fired in her life, Ophelia stormed over to the Hintons' sprawling mansion determined to give the team owner a piece of her mind. Who knew the man would actually capture a piece of her heart as well?

Ophelia slipped out of her gown, grabbed a satin hanger from the top of the towel rack, and hung the gown up on the back of the door. She admired the dress for a few minutes while her mind transformed the pink dress into a white wedding gown. *Mrs. Jonas Hinton.* She smiled. She could get used to that.

After Jonas gave his personal chef, Raul, the night's menu, he quickly found himself pacing the floor of his bedroom. So far, he'd only managed to remove his tuxedo jacket and loosen his tie. He wasn't at all thrilled with how the day's events had played out.

By all accounts, he should be a happy man. He had, after all, proposed to the woman of his dreams, albeit without a ring, and even though she'd said yes, he feared that he could actually lose her.

"Solomon Bassett," he spat, and then shook his head. Why hadn't he seen this coming? In the four months he'd been dating Ophelia, she'd talked of little else. There was always the time when she and Solomon did such-and-such or had a ball at this place or another. Hell, she'd actually managed to convince him that this guy was nothing more than a brother figure. But after what he saw today, that b.s. was no longer going to fly.

"But how in the hell am I going to keep those two apart?"

Chapter 4

Selma Parker pulled up to the Bassett estate and punched in the security code. She drummed her fingers impatiently on the steering wheel while she waited for the tall wrought-iron gate to creak open and allow her access to the property.

It had been a full week since a drunk Solomon had called and dropped the bomb about Ophelia's pending nuptials. Consequentially it had also been the last time she'd heard from him.

The moment the gate opened wide enough, Selma stepped on the accelerator and peeled down the long driveway.

"If he's not dead, I'm going to kill him," she vowed. During the past seven days, she had imagined every possible scenario as to why he wasn't returning her calls, and each one was worse than the last. "C'mon,

Selma. He wouldn't do anything stupid," said her inner voice of reason. Yet she wasn't entirely convinced.

She screeched to a halt, shut off her engine, and exited the car—almost at the same time. Seconds later, she hammered on the oak door like she was the police. When she didn't get a response, she took to playing musical numbers with the doorbell.

"I'm coming," came a bearlike growl.

She eased off the bell and jabbed her fists against her waist. When she heard the last of the three locks, she grabbed hold of the doorknob and forced her way into the house.

The door banged against something hard, and at Solomon's explosive expletive, she peeped around the heavy partition. "There you are!"

"If you say so," he mumbled, rubbing his head.

A dog's bark drew her attention, as well as the sound of paws slapping against hardwood floors.

"Brandy, don't you dare jump on my new suit," Selma snapped.

Reacting to the tone of her voice, Brandy stopped and cocked her head from side to side.

"It's good to know I'm not the only one afraid of you," Solomon said, closing the door.

"You *should* be scared." She popped him on the arm. "Having me all worried about you. Why haven't you returned any of my calls?"

"I've been busy." Solomon tightened the belt on his robe and shuffled past her.

"Busy my ass." She fell in line behind him. "Admit it. You've just been moping around here feeling sorry for yourself."

"If you came over to cheer me up, you're doing a lousy job."

"I'm not your damn cheerleading squad. I came be-cause—what in the hell—?" She stopped at the entry-way of the living room, but feeling something underfoot, she glanced down and kicked at an underwire bra.

"It was just a little party." Solomon plopped down on a nearby sofa.

Selma stepped away from the undergarment. "Some-thing tells me I need to spray this place down before I touch anything."

"Whatever." He tilted his head back and closed his eyes.

Tsking and shaking her head, Selma inched far-ther into the room while her gaze darted around. Ev-erything was covered in confetti, stringy things, beer cans, and plastic cups. "It must have been one hell of a party." From the corner of Selma's eyes, she noticed what looked like two bullet holes in the wall. "Please don't tell me your uncle Willy threw this party."

Solomon shrugged. "He was trying to cheer me up."

"I see it worked wonders." She sucked in an exasper-ated breath and tried to venture farther into the living room. "How long has this place been like this?" The moment she asked the question, Selma caught sight of Brandy eating leftover cake from off the coffee table. "Brandy, no!" She stepped over piles of only God knows what to shoo away the Doberman.

"Solomon, you can't let the dog eat this kind of stuff." She gathered up paper plates.

"Oh, it's not going to kill her," he grumbled.

"Maybe not, but Marcel will kill *you* if anything hap-pens to his dog." She turned sharply and grumbled the whole way to the kitchen, where more chaos loomed. The very thought of the kinds of germs lurking in the piles of dishes and strewn beer cans had Selma bolting from the room like an Olympian.

Returning to the living room, she was more than ready to give her friend a dose of tough love, but his pain-filled voice stopped her in her tracks.

"Selma, I really screwed things up."

Ophelia. It wasn't a hard conclusion to draw. "So how are you going to fix it?" she asked, unwilling to participate in a pity party.

Solomon didn't answer, but instead stared up at the cathedral ceilings as if waiting for a sign from above.

She jumped at the unexpected sound of giggling. In the next second, two scantily clad model types sauntered into the room. Selma immediately sucked in the small pouch around her waist and frowned at her physical opposites. "Sol, baby, Willy wants to know if you're coming back out to the pool?"

"He's busy," Selma snapped.

The women's gazes jumped to hers and then performed a slow drag over her attire. As if concluding that she wasn't a threat, sly smiles curled their lips.

"Hey, you're more than welcome to come out and join us if you want," one of them offered, undoubtedly knowing that she wouldn't.

"*I'm* busy, too."

"Tell my uncle I'll be out later," Solomon said. His gaze was still glued to the ceiling.

"Whatever you say, Sol, baby."

"Please stop calling me that," he said. "I hate that name."

The women shrugged and gave Selma a final once-over before they turned, with most of their butt cheeks hanging out, and walked out.

Selma rolled her eyes and marched to one of the

large windows. She pushed aside a long curtain panel and glanced out. The pool, about fifty yards from the main house, was crawling with half-dressed women.

"So this is how you're planning to get over Ophelia—surrounding yourself with a bunch of chickenheads?"

"It worked for the first twenty-four hours," he confessed.

She turned away from the window to see he still hadn't moved. 'So what's plan B?"

"Die of a broken heart, I guess." He huffed out a breath. "It seems to be working."

Her frown deepened as she stared at him. "I don't think I've met anyone more pathetic."

He dropped his head again and puffed out a long breath. "That's nice to know." He shook his head. "When she told me, I couldn't say anything," he said. "I just stood there."

"It was bound to happen," Selma said as gently as she could. However, her words just seemed to crush Solomon.

The phone rang. Solomon glanced over at the silver and black cordless.

"I'll get it." She rolled her eyes.

"It's her. Let the answering machine pick it up."

"How do you know it's her? It could be Marcel checking to see what a lousy job you're doing with Brandy."

"It's her. I just know it."

"Hey, Solomon, it's me," Ophelia's voice rang out from the answering machine.

Selma stiffened and glanced back at Solomon's I-told-you-so expression.

"I was just calling because I wanted to bounce some ideas off you about the wedding. We're thinking about having it at Château Élan. Won't that be great? Man, I still can't believe this is happening. Anyway, I really want you, Marcel, and Jonas to spend some time together. You know…try to make him feel like one of the gang. It would mean the world to me."

Solomon plopped his head back against the sofa again.

"So," Ophelia continued, "just give me a call on my cell when you get this message. Love you, bye."

Selma closed her eyes.

"Oh, by the way," Ophelia added. "We've moved the date up. We're now getting married in November. Isn't that great? Okay, bye. Call me."

After the loud click, the living room filled with an awkward silence.

In Selma's mind, she ran through a short list of things she could say, should say, but she knew none of it was going to help ease her friend's pain.

"Selma?" Solomon croaked.

"Yes?"

"Could you please just shoot me?"

Ophelia stared at the phone long after she hung up. She couldn't shake the feeling that Solomon was home but had chosen not to answer.

The doorbell rang and broke her trance.

Pushing the incident to the back of her mind, she raced through the condominium, wondering if Jonas had forgotten his key. But when she jerked open the front door, she was taken aback at the sight of her mother, Isabella, and her good friend and Delta sister, Kailua.

The three of them screamed.

"What are you two doing here?" Ophelia finally asked when her mother's arms wrapped around her.

"You're engaged!" her mother announced while

squeezing a little tighter and bouncing on her toes. "I'm so excited for you."

Ophelia's excitement dropped a notch. She hadn't told her mother the news, so Jonas must have. Why hadn't he waited until they could tell her parents together? "I—I'm so happy that you came." She finally eased her mother out of her arms and accepted her friend's embrace.

"Well, I don't know about anybody else, but I'm still in shock," Kailua said, delivering a quick peck to Ophelia's cheek.

"What do you mean?"

Isabella quickly gave the young woman a reproachful glare. "Nothing. She doesn't mean anything."

Ophelia pulled back and stared into eyes that so closely resembled her own. However, her mother was a professional at dodging taboo subjects.

"Your father is out of town on business but sends his love. He should be back Thursday."

She nodded. "Well, I—I sort of hoped Jonas and I would tell you and dad together."

Her mother promptly shooed off her concerns. "Don't blame Jonas. I practically dragged the information out of him when I called here this morning."

"You called?"

"Yes, dear. I wanted to know how Marcel's wedding went, but Jonas said that you were still sleeping. Separate beds, I hope."

Kailua nearly choked trying to stifle her laughter.

"As a matter of fact, yes." Ophelia closed the door and then led them into the condo.

"Baby, where's the bathroom?" her mother asked.

Ophelia directed her to the hallway. "Straight down.

Last door on your right." She smiled and then returned to the living room.

Kailua waltzed around and whistled impressively. "Hot damn! You always seem to hit the jackpot."

"I don't know about that." Ophelia laughed awkwardly.

Her Delta sister shook her head while she ran her hand along the sofa's soft Italian leather. "It must be nice having your choice of millionaires just waiting at the tips of your fingers."

"And what is that supposed to mean?"

A beautiful smile bloomed across Kailua's full, shapely lips. "I mean Solomon, of course. You can't tell me he doesn't have a few bucks in the bank."

A chilling and awkward moment passed between the two women.

"C'mon, girl." Kailua smacked her playfully, and painfully, on the arm. "You can't blame your girl for being just a little envious."

Ophelia rolled her eyes as her smile widened. "I wish everyone would just stop with that."

"Uh-huh."

"I mean it." Ophelia shrugged. "Besides, Solomon is a great friend, but dating? I like the strong, aggressive type. Solomon is quiet and sensitive. It would have never worked. We're better off as friends. Yeah."

Kailua's lips curled upward as she folded her arms. "Are you trying to convince me or yourself?"

"I'm not trying to convince anybody. I'm just stating a fact. Solomon and I are friends. Period."

"Good." Kailua unfolded her arms. "Then you won't mind if I just take him off your hands for you."

Ophelia blinked.

Kailua continued. "He's available. I'm available… and you're off the market. Right?"

Swallowing a painful lump, Ophelia croaked her reply. "Right."

Chapter 5

After surviving another week, Solomon was finally tired of being sick and tired. Plus the cops had warned him that if they had to come out to his place for another noise ordinance violation, they were going to start hauling people to jail. So he kicked his beloved uncle Willy and his harem of ghetto-fabulous women to the curb.

Selma happily hired and supervised a cleaning crew to scrub and sanitize every nook and cranny of the house, while Solomon forced himself back into his old routine. If he just kept busy, he reasoned, then the days wouldn't seem so long, and his heart wouldn't feel so heavy.

Jonas and I have been dating for a while, and last night he popped the question.

He shook the sound of Ophelia's voice from his head and pushed himself to complete another mile during his morning run. Yes, yes, he had had plenty of opportunities to tell Ophelia how he felt. But the truth of the matter was there never had really been a good time.

The moment puberty hit and Ophelia transformed into a beautiful swan, she was the object of desire of every boy in the neighborhood. Yeah, she hung out with him and Marcel, but Solomon honestly believed it was simply because she had the hots for Marcel.

And no matter what Marcel said now, there was a time when Marcel was smitten by their friend's long, tanned legs and perfect hourglass figure, too.

Though he'd promised to stop dwelling on the past, Solomon's mind replayed the last two and a half decades, particularly the times that included the woman of his dreams. They were about thirteen when Ophelia suddenly was boy crazy. To this day he remembered the names of each boy she ogled or fantasized marrying.

Attacking a steep hill with Brandy at his heels, Solomon's thoughts returned to a day he would never forget....

Ten Minutes in Heaven

Chapter 6

Atlanta, Georgia, June 1982

"Why do we have to go over to Lisa's house?" eleven-year-old Solomon Bassett whined, snatching off his baseball cap. "We're supposed to be going to practice."

A sly grin sloped Marcel's lips as he draped his arm around Solomon's shoulders. "Didn't you hear how many girls are going to be over at Lisa's party?"

Solomon's face twisted in disgust. "Girls? Why on earth do you want to go play with a bunch of silly girls?"

Marcel's eyes widened. "Please tell me you're kidding."

Solomon stopped in his tracks and kicked at the dirt. He didn't want to go. Whenever he got around girls, he turned into a bumbling idiot or a stumbling klutz. He was nothing like his best friend, Marcel, who always seemed to make the girls bat their eyelashes and go on nonstop giggling sprees.

Marcel leaned closer and whispered, "Lisa promised they'll be playing ten minutes in heaven." He wiggled his eyebrows.

Solomon cringed. Ten minutes locked in a closet with a girl didn't sound like heaven. "I don't know," he hedged, and then he remembered something. "I thought Lisa's father warned you to stay away from her?"

"He's away on business." Marcel slapped Solomon hard across his back. "Besides, Lisa's *mother* thinks I'm harmless and adorable. C'mon." Marcel slapped his back again. "I promise you're going to have the time of your life."

Solomon doubted it.

Minutes later, Solomon and Marcel arrived at the home of McCarthy Junior High School's most popular girl—Lisa Simpson. Lisa was a pretty mixed-race girl with what most kids called good hair, mainly because she had Indian in her family—according to her. Most of the boys in the neighborhood liked her; however, she'd made it clear she'd set her sights on Marcel.

Solomon shuffled into the house and, just as he expected, all the girls flocked around his buddy. Well, not all of them. The new girl, Ophelia Missler, just hovered around the punch bowl and scowled at everyone.

Solomon didn't like her. Her family had moved into the neighborhood this past winter, and so far, she spent most her time acting like she was better than everybody else. He liked to call her Miss Smarty Pants because she loved to rattle off useless information like one of those Apple computers his father owned. Actually, she could throw a better slider than Solomon...and she could run circles around him.

His gaze lowered to her long, bony legs, and he was instantly reminded of a giraffe. No wonder she was fast.

She pushed up her glasses, which only magnified her strange-colored eyes. As usual, her thick, dusty brown hair was split down the middle, and two large twisted ponytails hung on the sides of her face. It didn't help that Ophelia also had enough wire in her mouth to fence in Solomon's backyard. She was no competition for Lisa or her close-knit gal pals.

Drawing a deep breath, he glanced around the room and spotted a couple of other guys who were doing a great job holding up the walls. No way was he going to have a good time at this place. Everything was pink and frilly and giving him a headache.

A chorus of giggles erupted from behind him, and he glanced back in time to see his buddy turn up his thumbs like the Fonz. Marcel was the master.

Shaking his head, Solomon drifted across the room toward Ophelia. "Mind if I have some punch?"

Her eyes landed on him, and then rolled toward the ceiling. "I guess. It's a free country."

He frowned. *What the heck was her problem?*

"Okay, everybody gather around," Lisa broadcast. "It's time to play ten minutes in heaven."

Solomon didn't move.

Neither did Ophelia.

Lisa grabbed two jars from the table. "Did everyone place their name in the right jar?"

Solomon relaxed. Since he didn't put his name in the jar, there was no way he was going to be called.

"I can't believe my mom made me come to this stupid party," Ophelia mumbled.

"Why did your mom *make* you come?" Solomon asked.

Ophelia's bored gaze once again fell on him. "Because Lisa and I are cousins," she informed him dully.

"O-oh." Solomon nodded and glanced back over at Lisa. He saw no family resemblance.

Lisa clapped. "Okay, the first boy's name is…" She reached a hand inside one of the jars. "…Marcel."

"No surprise there," Solomon grumbled. To his surprise, Ophelia snickered.

"…and Sabrina," Lisa announced.

Everyone oohed and aahed the chosen couple and then broke out into a chorus of "Marcel and Sabrina sitting in a tree. K-I-S-S-I-N-G."

It was all so childish, but at the same time, Solomon couldn't help but be envious of his friend. Sabrina, after all, looked like Penny from *Good Times*.

The moment Lisa closed the door, everyone else gathered around. After a few minutes, they all started to back away, complaining that they couldn't hear anything.

Ten minutes later, Marcel and Sabrina emerged with mussed hair and wide grins.

Solomon shook his head and just marveled at his newfound idol.

"It's sickening how they throw themselves at him," Ophelia mumbled with disgust.

"What—are you jealous or something?" Solomon asked, cocking his head.

"Hardly."

He didn't buy it. All the girls were crazy about Marcel. And as far as he could tell, she was no different.

The game continued. Solomon lost count of the number of times Marcel's name was drawn. Each time he was paired with a different girl. *Lucky devil.*

Just when Solomon thought he'd explode if he took another sip of punch, all eyes turned toward him.

"What?"

Lisa waved a thin strip of paper. "I pulled your name."

"You couldn't have. I didn't…" His eyes cut to a smiling and winking Marcel. "That's all right, guys. I don't want to play."

Lisa balled up her hands and jabbed them into her waist. "You have to play. I pulled your name."

This was another reason why Solomon didn't care for girls. They were always determined to get their way.

Solomon was not intimidated and was more than ready to lock horns with a potential bully when Marcel and a few of the other guys grabbed him and hauled him toward the closet.

"Guys, stop. Wait a minute."

Lisa beamed happily and plunged her hand into the other jar. "And the lucky girl is…Ophelia."

Solomon's protests were nothing compared to Ophelia's, and surprisingly, it took more people to get the leggy tomboy shoved into the closet.

Finally, the door slammed on Ophelia's menacing threats and wild rantings. However, than didn't stop her from pounding on the door or rattling the knob.

Solomon was amused. "You might as well give up. They're not going to let us out of here until our time is up."

"Shut up…and stay away from me."

"You got it."

On the other side of the door, a loud chorus of "Solomon and Ophelia sitting in a tree. K-I-S-S-I-N-G," rang out.

"I bet you think this is funny," she snapped.

"I do now."

"Well, I don't. And I'm not kissing you."

"That's good to know." He sat on the floor, content to just wait the ten minutes out.

"Wait until my father hears about this. He's going to skin you alive."

"Whoa. Wait. I'm not happy about this either. You're the last person I want to be stuck in a closet with."

He couldn't see her, but he could hear her draw in an angry breath.

"And what is wrong with me?"

Was she for real?

"Well?"

"N-nothing. It's just that...you're not exactly my type."

"*You* have a type?"

Now he was insulted. "I don't know why I'm even talking to you."

"Because I'm the only one in here, Einstein." She plopped down beside him.

When her bony legs brushed against his, he flinched and then wondered why.

"Relax," she sneered. "I'm not going to bite you."

"No. You're just going to sic your father on me...for *not* kissing you." Silence trailed his words. "Not that I want to."

"But you're thinking about it."

"Am not." He rolled his eyes.

"Uh-huh. My Dad told me that boys think about it all the time."

"Think about what?"

"You know—*it*."

Solomon frowned. "You don't know what *it* is, do

you?" Her silence was his answer. He rocked back with laughter. "Miss Smarty Pants doesn't know anything."

"Whatever."

"Admit it."

"No."

He rolled his eyes and waited. However, he never knew ten minutes lasted so long.

"We have about five more minutes," she said, glancing at a glow-in-the-dark Mickey Mouse watch.

He exhaled and nodded, but as time ticked on, he wondered what he was going to tell everyone when they were finally out of there. If he came out saying that nothing happened, what would that do to his reputation? Not that he had one. He didn't want to develop one of being unable to score with someone like Ophelia. "So, what are you going to tell them when we get out?" he asked.

"Tell them?"

"Yeah." He shrugged. "Everyone is going to wonder what happened in here."

"I'm telling them the truth. Nothing happened."

"Of course. Right." He nodded. That was probably the right thing to do, he concluded, and then allowed the silence to stretch between them once again.

"What are you going to tell them?" she asked almost timidly.

"Well, I guess the same thing you are."

Silence.

"You think we'll get laughed at?"

"It's almost a certainty," he said, with a cloud of gloom and doom hanging over his head. Suddenly, this seemed like a no-win situation, and he was going to be the loser no matter what. He heard her turn toward him.

"Then kiss me."

"What? Gross."

"Look. The other girls already make fun of me because I like to play sports. I'm not leaving here letting them think that they can do something I can't. So kiss me." She grabbed his shirt and yanked him forward.

Great. She was stronger than he was, too. Whatever protest Solomon had died the moment his lips landed on hers. Surprisingly soft, her mouth tasted like Strawberry Bubble Yum, and her skin was just as soft as his newborn sister's. Although he had nothing to compare it to, he was fairly certain that she was the best kisser in the entire world…no, the galaxy…or better yet, the whole universe.

His entire body was doing funny things, and his head…well, it was getting hard to think clearly. He hated to admit it, even to himself, but he liked kissing Ophelia Missler. He liked it a lot.

Neither heard when the door opened, but both sprung apart when a chorus of laughter erupted from the party. Within seconds, they were pulled in different directions. Solomon received his fair share of pats on the back and idol worshipping. However, his gaze kept darting across the room to the person who'd just changed his life—the girl he would love forever: Ophelia Missler.

Solomon stopped running when he reached his front door and tilted forward as if that would help get air into his lungs. His chest hurt to the point that he thought he was having a heart attack.

"Are you finished trying to kill yourself?" Selma asked, stepping out of the house.

He ignored the question and tried to massage away the stabbing pain.

"Whoa. I was just joking," she said. "Are you all right?"

He shook his head, but then changed his mind. "I'm fine. My age is just creeping up on me, that's all." He glanced at her and could tell she wasn't buying it. "I'm hopping in the shower and going to work."

Selma's brows lifted in surprise. "Are you up to it?"

"I need to do something before I lose my mind." He stepped past her and entered the house. Still panting, he crossed the foyer and was starting up the stairs when he suddenly turned to face her. "If I haven't said it in the last week, thanks for coming to my rescue. Who knows how far I would have sunk if you hadn't come over and taken charge."

A genuine smile spread across Selma's face. "Hey, that's what friends are for. But if you want to reward me, you can take me to dinner. I head back to New York tomorrow. I have a group performing on David Letterman."

"You got yourself a date." He winked, turned, and jogged up the rest of the stairs.

An hour later, Solomon arrived at T & B Entertainment. He rushed in and shared smiles with several of the company's female employees. Women made up 92 percent of the staff. This was attributable to Marcel's desire to surround himself with all things beautiful. As long as everyone was competent in their jobs, Solomon didn't mind the eye candy.

Before heading down to his own office, he made a detour to visit Marcel's new secretary, Zandra Holloway. Zandra was sixty-two, and frankly, Solomon didn't know whether things were going to work out with the new employee. She was much too jumpy for his liking, and she never seemed to remember where she placed anything.

"Good afternoon, Zandra."

As usual, the fragile-looking woman nearly jumped out of her skin and sloshed coffee around. "Oh, Solomon."

He frowned.

"I mean, Mr. Bassett. I didn't see you come in."

"It's okay. No need to get up. I just came to see how everything was going."

"Couldn't be better," she rushed to answer.

Another glance at her cluttered desk and doubt began to surface. "All right. Just remember Chelsea can help you with whatever you need."

A wide smile stretched across her thick lips. Again Solomon was struck by the thought that Zandra belonged in a kitchen, baking cookies for a neighborhood of children.

Minutes later, Solomon headed toward his own office. When his secretary, Chelsea, saw him, she pulled a phone from her ear and covered the mouthpiece with her hand. "Ms. Missler is waiting in your office."

Solomon froze.

"Is there something wrong?" Chelsea asked.

"No." He fluttered a smile in her direction and then pushed open his door.

Nestled in the center of his burgundy leather couch, Ophelia glanced up from her magazine and hit him with her high-wattage smile. "There you are." She stood and crossed the room. "If I didn't know any better, I'd swear you were avoiding me." She delivered a quick peck on the side of his cheek.

Solomon's heart hammered against his chest. "Don't be silly. I've been busy."

Her beautiful golden eyes widened. "Too busy to help your best friend plan her wedding?"

"What can I say?" He stepped back, needing the space to clear his thoughts. "I've been doing double duty while Marcel is on his honeymoon," he lied smoothly. "Besides, what do I know about weddings? Just tell me the time and place, and I'll be there." He hoped she didn't notice how much his chuckle sounded like a misfired weapon.

No such luck.

She studied him. "You still don't like Jonas, do you?"

He settled behind his desk, and avoided meeting her gaze. "Don't be silly. I don't know the man. If you like him, then I love him."

"Good." Ophelia followed him and rested her hip against his desk. "Join us for dinner tonight."

Solomon opened his mouth.

"No excuses," she added, pointing a finger. "You have to help me squash this nonsense with Jonas that there's something going on between me and you."

He blinked. "What do you mean?"

She shrugged and rolled her eyes. "Jonas is of the opinion that women and men can't be friends without the man having a hidden agenda."

More stilted laughter rumbled from his chest while his gaze struggled to find a resting place.

"So, you'll come?"

He finally made a fatal mistake and looked at her. Her golden gaze immediately imprisoned him. How could he ever refuse her anything?

"It would help if you had a date, though. And believe it or not, I can help you there. You remember my friend Kailua?"

"That's no necessary. I already have a date," he said casually, thinking of his plans with Selma.

"You do?" She blinked. "What's with you and Marcel holding out on me?"

He rocked back into his chair. What harm would it do for her to think he was involved with someone? Between her and Marcel, he was beginning to look like a sad case indeed. "Look's who's calling the kettle black."

"Touché." She rolled her eyes and bedazzled him with another smile. "So who is she?"

He hesitated, but then thought that his good friend would be more than glad to help him out of a jam. "Her name is Selma Parker. I've mentioned her before."

Ophelia blinked. "Oh."

"Is something wrong?"

"No," she recovered quickly. "No, no. Not at all." She glanced down and then frowned at him. "It's just that whenever you've talked about Selma in the past, I always thought she was…married."

Damn, he'd forgotten about that. "Uh, yeah. She… is…married." He folded his arms and waited for his brain to kick into gear and give him something else to say; however, nothing ever came.

"Oh?" Ophelia's eyes widened as she slowly moved away from his desk. "I see."

"Uh, you know," he tried to explain, but still nothing came. "Maybe it's not a good idea if we join—"

"No, no. I mean if this is something…uh, well, I mean, I still want you two to come."

Damn. "I don't know, Ophelia."

"Please, Sol."

He tensed at the pet name only she was allowed to use.

"I'm not leaving until you say you're coming."

He hesitated and then finally huffed out, "All right. We'll come. But about Selma—"

"No, it's okay," she continued with an awkward smile. "I'm not judging. If you like her, then I love her."

Chapter 7

"He hasn't bought you a ring yet?" Kailua asked, lifting her gaze from the rack of wedding gowns. "You have to be kidding me."

Ophelia shrugged, not sure why she even mentioned it. "He'll get around to it. I mean...the proposal was sort of an impromptu kind of thing anyway." She scanned through the rack across from her friend.

Kailua's brows rose. "What the hell does that mean? He didn't think this thing through?"

"No... I mean, yes." Ophelia rolled her eyes. "I just mean...we're getting married." She flashed a smile and turned toward yet another rack of dresses.

"Well, I'm glad you cleared that up." Kailua glided next to her. "But why don't you tell me about this mysterious impromptu proposal?"

Ophelia didn't understand her own flash of annoyance. She was, after all, the one who had brought it up.

The thing most heavily on her mind was Solomon—him and his *married* girlfriend.

Kailua tapped her shoulder. "Hello?"

Suddenly snapped back to reality, Ophelia drew a deep breath. "What? Oh, yeah. It was beautiful. We went to dinner at San Pedro's. Girl, the place was off the chain. I even managed to get in some salsa moves—"

"I thought Jonas didn't dance?"

"He doesn't. But there were a few men on hand."

Kailua chuckled.

"What?"

"Nothing." Kailua shook her head. "I didn't mean to interrupt. Go ahead on with your story."

Ophelia didn't want to, especially if it was going to be subjected to Kailua's biting ridicule and sarcastic commentary.

"Continue," Kailua prompted.

"Well, after dinner I told him about Marcel and Diana…and I think I was telling him how incredibly romantic their whole love story sounded. It was truly a page out of a fairy tale." Ophelia sighed. "Nothing even remotely like that ever happens to me. Then again, Marcel could charm the habit off a nun."

"Yeah. I remember him. His wife is one lucky woman. But cut me a break. Men drool after you all the time. Trust me. More than half the men I dated in college were using me to get to you."

"Stop it." Ophelia playfully elbowed Kailua in the side and glanced up to make sure that her mother was still out of earshot.

"I ain't lying. Hell, if it wasn't for them, I would've been stuck in the sorority house every Friday and Saturday night dying my hair different colors."

"What are you talking about? You're beautiful. You didn't need me to get dates."

"Thanks." Kailua flashed a half smile. "But you've apparently forgotten how many chins I had back in the day."

"You were still beautiful. And believe me, I went through my own ugly-duckling phase."

"You keep telling me that. But until I see pictures, I don't believe any of it."

Ophelia laughed. "Then don't believe it, because I'm pretty sure I've burned all of those damn things."

"Figures." Kailua rolled her eyes and for the next few minutes the women did what they did best in silence: shop.

"Oh, look at this one." Kailua pulled out a beautiful white gown with delicate beading around the bodice and waistline.

"Ooh. That is nice. But you know an A-line on these hips makes me look fat, and my cousins are going to need a little more support than that. Let's not forget that I'm going to be dancing and everything. We don't want them bouncing around in everyone's face."

"Good point. What size are those babies anyway?"

"34D."

Kailua glanced down at her padded B cup and shook her head. "That's all right. I'm saving up for a new pair." She slid the gown back onto the rack. "After that, everywhere I go I'm going to be buck naked. Watch and see."

Ophelia laughed. "You're crazy enough to do it, too." She shook her head. "You know, even if men were falling all over me as you say, none of them approached me. Hell, before Jonas, I went a whole year without a date. You know that."

"That's because you're too picky. He's too short, he's

too tall—you always find something wrong with a guy instead of giving him a chance."

"Not true. Unlike you, I just refuse to jump on any-thing that moves." Ophelia gave Kailua a tight smile and beamed with satisfaction for getting in her own jibe. *Married.* "Anyway, after I told Jonas the story, he got very quiet and then reached for my hand." A lazy smile drifted across Ophelia's lips.

"He was so cute…and *nervous.* I think that was what clued me in that something was up. Suddenly, I had this big ball of anxiety sitting in the pit of my stomach, and I couldn't quite get enough air in my lungs. For a split second there, I didn't want him to say it. I wanted to snatch my hand back and run like hell, but then I got to thinking—Jonas is a handsome, successful man who adores me. What else could a woman want?"

"Let's not forget *rich,*" Kailua added smugly. "Chile, you can kick off your working shoes and fill up your days with spas, massages, and shopping. I know that's what I would do."

For the millionth time, Ophelia wondered just how she and Kailua had managed to be good friends.

"Maids, chefs, shopping sprees…and you better not forget your homegirl." Kailua jabbed her thumb at the center of her chest. "A sistah is a little tired of being broke, ya know?"

"Maybe if you'd lay off of Mr. Visa and Mr. Master-Card every once in a while."

Horror blazed Kailua's eyes.

"It was just a suggestion." Ophelia shrugged with a light smile. "Well, I'm sorry to burst your bubble, but I intend to keep working," Ophelia said, moving to yet another rack of dresses, even though she was convinced that she wasn't going to find what she was looking for anyway. "Just as soon as I find a new job. I'll probably wait until after the wedding now."

"Why in the hell would you keep working?"

"I don't know. Maybe because I *enjoy* it?" She pulled her purse strap higher over her shoulder. "I got a great sense of accomplishment working at the center. I loved it."

"And what's not to love about being pampered all day?"

Ophelia shook her head. "Don't blow a coronary. It's just not my style. I feel like I'm making a difference with my work. I dedicated the past eleven years to making that rehabilitation center a success—until my fiancée put me out of business. But I'll always work. And I don't think Solomon expects me to just stay home. He loves me and knows how much my work means to me."

Married.

Kailua stopped and looked at her.

"What?"

"Nothing." Kailua's eyes twinkled above her wide smile. "Nothing at all."

Jonas spent the past six hours planted in a plush chair in the back of the upscale Opulence jewelry store. He was on a mission to find the perfect diamond, and now he was no closer than when he had started. He needed something exquisite—something that complemented his fiancée's unique beauty and would stand out.

"Champagne, Mr. Hinton?" a pretty saleswoman offered from a silver tray.

"No, thank you." He flashed a smile and then stood when a distinguished-looking gentleman entered the room. In the next second, Jonas recognized the man only because he was the spitting image of the previous owner, who was no doubt his father. But Jonas still held his tongue because he knew the man also had a twin.

"Mr. Hinton," the man said. "I'm Malcolm Williams, president of Opulence. I just happened to be in the store today when I learned of your visit."

"Ah, Mr. Williams." Jonas's smile widened as he accepted the man's handshake. "I knew your father, Noah, when he was running the company. My condolences on his passing."

"Thank you. It's been a few years, but he's still terribly missed." Williams's amicable smile held as he drew a deep breath and slapped his hands together. "So I hear you're shopping for an engagement ring. I take it congratulations are in order?"

"Yes, yes. Thank you. I sort of put the cart before the horse in asking before getting the ring. But hey, I guess it's a sign of a good woman that she said 'yes' anyway."

"Hear, hear! Then again, you're talking to a man whose wife proposed to him."

The room swelled with laughter as another saleswoman appeared with another tray of diamonds. A few stones instantly grabbed Jonas's attention.

"I figured you might like to take a look at these precious gems. I don't think you'll be disappointed." Williams gestured to Jonas's stunning new choices. "We keep these reserved for a few of our special clients."

Being a man who took pride in knowing a good thing when he saw it, Jonas's mood brightened considerably. "Now this is more like it." He sat back into the plush chair and reached for a magnificent, vivid, blue pear-shaped diamond.

"Ah, I see you have exquisite taste, Mr. Hinton. As you can see, that diamond is a Cartier-style pear cut with a total weight of two carats."

"It's perfect." Jonas accepted the magnifying loupe and place it over his right eye to study the diamond's detail. "She's going to love this."

The room fell silent during his long inspection. He loved everything about the unique gem; and in his mind's eye, he envisioned Ophelia's exuberant reaction. This ring would erase all those silly notions of abstinence until their wedding night.

"I'll take it. I'll need it in a size six platinum setting."

Williams nodded. "Very well. Sally here will take care of the size for you, and if you'll follow me, we can initiate the wire transfer."

Jonas stood. "By the way, and yes, I know this is a rather strange question, but you wouldn't happen to know where there's a good dance school for adults? Better yet, someone who may be interested in giving private lessons?"

One of Williams's neatly groomed brows arched.

"My fiancée loves to dance," Jonas felt compelled to explain. "And I have two left feet. So I thought it would be nice to, sort of, surprise her and actually know what I'm doing when I dance with her on our wedding day."

Williams smiled. "She really must be some woman."

"You have no idea."

"In that case, I think I can help you out in that area as well. Follow me."

Jonas's excitement about the ring literally had him walking with an extra bounce in his step. He couldn't wait until tonight when he finally presented Ophelia with her engagement ring.

Chapter 8

No matter how hard Solomon tried, he simply couldn't focus on work. He canceled one meeting after another and couldn't summon the slightest sympathy for Chelsea, who had to clean up Zandra's screwups. For the umpteenth time that day, his exhausted secretary entered his office and caught him staring out of the window daydreaming.

"I need a raise," she announced curtly, plopping a stack of folders on the corner of his desk.

"So you keep telling me," he grinned slyly.

"You better pick up the hint before you end up with someone like Zandra working for you."

He cringed. "It's not getting any better?"

Chelsea rolled her eyes. "Frankly, I think Diana picked this woman as the most unlikely woman to hit on her man."

Solomon nodded. The thought had occurred to him, too.

A soft double rap on the door drew their attention, and before either of them could command the visitor to enter, the door bolted open.

"There's my favorite nephew!" Willy's voice boomed into the office as a wide smile monopolized his face.

Chelsea looked physically ill. "I'm out of here."

"Whoa. Where's the fire?" Willy puffed up his chest as his twinkling gaze soaked in her profile. "I see you still don't have a ring around that finger. You know I could change all of that." He winked.

"Not if you were the last Negro—"

"Chelsea," Solomon sliced into the conversation. "That will be all."

Undaunted, Willy's smile only grew wider. "I like them feisty."

"I guess that explains why you hooked up with Nora Gibson," she added.

"Jealous?" He spread out his arms. "If you like what you see, fight for it, baby."

Chelsea gave him the universal brick wall sign and headed for the door. "I'm out of here. It's five o'clock, and I don't do overtime."

"I'll make a note of that in your next evaluation." Solomon beamed a smile at her, and it had the same effect as if he'd done so in the face of a starving tiger.

"You're not funny," she sassed and turned on her heels.

"C'mon and drop it like it's hot one time for me." Willy chuckled.

She rolled her eyes and kept moving.

Willy blew a kiss at her back, and then released a hearty laugh when the door slammed closed behind her.

"Why do you insist on pissing her off?"

"Cuz I can." He winked again and then made himself

comfortable in the chair in front of Solomon's desk. "I see you're feeling better. Didn't I tell you there's nothing like a house full of women backing it up to put a smile on your face?"

Solomon had to laugh. "Well, it must have worked," he said, unwilling to rain on his uncle's parade.

"Good, good. I was afraid that Selma chick had ruined things for you. Who is she, anyway?"

"Just a good friend of mine. We've known each other for about seven years now. She's an entertainment lawyer and represents a few of our groups."

"Humph. She acts more like your wife by the way she was bossin' everyone out of there."

Solomon laughed at the direction their conversation had taken. "She's somebody's wife, just not mine." He could tell his uncle's interest had been piqued by the way he stroked his chin.

"Married, huh? Well, she's still an attractive woman—little meat on her bones, but I can give her a good workout."

"Do you ever turn that off?"

"What do you mean?" Willy asked.

"Everything leads to sexual innuendo with you. Do you ever think of anything else?"

"Money. But I have plenty of that, too." His laugh filled the room. "Come on, relax. I just like to have a good time."

"All the time?"

"Life is short, nephew. You should know that better than anyone."

The reference to Solomon's father wasn't hard to make. Solomon would be lying if he didn't admit a fear of dying like his father had, at the age of forty-nine.

"I have a couple of eager beavers lined up tonight. What do you say? I told them all about you."

"Thanks, but no thanks. I already have plans." Not to mention he was starting to be a little creeped out that his uncle was finding him dates.

"Cancel them."

"Can't."

"Can't means 'I don't want to.'"

"Fine. I don't want to. I'm taking Selma over to Ophelia's tonight."

Willy appeared speechless for a moment—a rare occurrence. "Why, you sly dog," he thundered. "Creeping with a married woman. I knew you had it in you. We are related, after all."

"No, no. It's—"

"Hey, hey. You don't have to explain nothing to me. I'm a slick cat from way back. 'Tween you and me, there ain't nothing like a married woman. Am I right?"

Solomon frowned. "Please tell me you're neutered."

Willy just laughed and reached inside his jacket for his trademark Cuban cigars.

"No smoking in here."

Willy ignored him and lit up. "You can make an exception for your favorite uncle, can't you?" Willy puffed out a small cloud.

Solomon squashed his annoyance.

"Great." His uncle's attention advanced to one of the silver-framed photographs nestled on the corner of his desk. "Ah, check her out," he said, ogling Ophelia. "I never did understand why you didn't get with this pretty filly. Everyone knows you two have a thang for each other."

"What?" Solomon's eyes rounded. He'd never told

Willy anything about his feelings toward his best friend—mainly because his uncle had a big mouth.

"C'mon. I might be getting old, but there's nothing wrong with my eyes."

Solomon suddenly glanced at his watch. "Hey, look at the time. I guess I better get going."

"Oh, what's your hurry?"

Standing, Solomon reached for his jacket from the corner hook and quickly slid his arms through the sleeves. "I have dinner plans, remember?"

"Ah, I must have touched a nerve."

"No, I just don't want to be late."

"Uh-huh." Willy didn't attempt to get up, nor did he place the picture back down on the desk. "I know this question is a little late, but who was the chick you were trying to drink out of your system the past couple of weeks?" He met Solomon's gaze. "And try to be honest."

Solomon held on to his stiff smile and headed out. "I'll never tell, old man." He pulled open the door and was surprised to see Selma.

"Oh." She smiled. "Perfect timing."

"Ah, if it isn't the old ball and chain," Willy said, finally setting the picture down and pushing his way out of the chair. "I'm surprised I recognized you without a Black & Decker in your hand."

"And you without a group of porno star rejects."

"Sassy." He winked at Solomon. "I can see the attraction."

"I'll catch you later, Uncle Willy."

"Fine by me. I'll give you two some privacy." He winked again. "We'll talk later."

"I'm looking forward to it," Solomon replied.

"You know, Selma, you should come to one of my parties some time."

"And hang out while you liquor up underage hooch-ies?"

"Hey, everyone knows my motto—you have to be eighteen to come, but twenty-one to swallow."

Solomon groaned. "And on that note, we'll be seeing you, uncle."

Selma managed to keep it together until the door finally closed. "That man is off the chain. How on earth do you put up with him?"

"He grows on you."

"Yeah…like fungus." She chuckled, and quickly changed the subject. "I decided where you're taking me for dinner."

"Uh, about that."

Selma moaned and dropped her head back. "Don't tell me you're backing out."

"No, no. We're still going to dinner…but there are a few things you need to know first."

An angry Jonas paced outside the bathroom door. "I can't believe you invited him to dinner," he barked.

"I don't see what the big deal is," Ophelia responded nonchalantly.

"Of course you don't," he mumbled, but then he shouted back through the door. "I, kind of, had a romantic evening planned for just the two of us." He paused and shook his head. "I mean, can't you call him and cancel?"

The door opened and Ophelia stepped out, wearing a red dress that lovingly hugged her curves. Jonas's jaw slacked as suspicion crawled around the back of his brain.

"Don't be silly." Ophelia tilted her head to slide on a

pair of earrings. "I can't cancel now. They're probably on the way over."

"Why are you wearing that?" He paused. "Did you say *they?*"

She dropped her gaze to her dress. "What's wrong with what I have on?"

"You said *they,*" he repeated.

Looking back up, Ophelia frowned, and then walked over to the dresser mirror. "Solomon is bringing his girlfriend." She twirled around and examined every angle. "You don't like this dress?"

Jonas blinked and stilled his excitement until he made sure he understood what he'd heard. "Solomon has a girlfriend?"

She faced him again with a look of incredulity. "And why wouldn't he have a girlfriend? He's a handsome, charming, and successful man. I'm sure he has plenty of women begging for his attention."

"Okay. That was a little more than I asked for." He folded his arms and ignored the crawling sensation in the back of his head. "I'm just surprised. You never mentioned he had a girlfriend." *Was I wrong about this guy?*

"Well," she said, turning toward the mirror again, "I guess it's because I just found out today. Course, I was also the last to know about Marcel getting married. But, hey, I'm not complaining." She inspected her figure again and flapped her arms down at her side. "You're right, this dress makes my butt look too big. I'm going to change."

Jonas frowned. "I didn't say—"

"Oh, I know. I can wear that bright blue number you liked."

Remembering the ring in his pocket, he nodded with a crooked smile. "Yes, I love blue on you."

"Humph. You're about the only one. My mom says it does nothing for me."

"You don't like blue?"

"Oh, what about that fuchsia Chanel dress I bought yesterday? Solomon always said I looked good in that color."

"Did he now?" Jonas jammed his hands into his pockets to hide how they had curled in irritation.

Ophelia pulled the dress off the rack and showed it to him. "What do you think?"

"I hate purple."

"It's fuchsia."

"It's purple."

The sound of the doorbell jingling throughout the house halted his next words, which would've surely led to an argument.

"They're here." Ophelia fretted and turned back to her rack of clothes. "Go ahead and greet them," she instructed, seeming unaware of his rising anger. "I'll be down in a minute."

The bell rang again.

"Honey." Ophelia turned and blew him a kiss. "Now, go. Go. Go."

Amazingly, the airborne kiss was enough to cool his temper. Besides, he no longer had to worry. Solomon was coming to dinner with his girlfriend. *Girlfriend.*

He exited the bedroom with a sudden spring to his step. As he crossed through the living room, he heard the low hum of voices in the foyer. He rounded the corner just as Benton, his butler, accepted the couple's jackets.

"Good evening," Jonas greeted him with outstretched

arms, but his gaze immediately sought the ebony beauty at Solomon's side.

"Good evening," they replied.

"I can't tell you how much of a pleasure it is to meet you...?"

"Selma," she supplied her name, and then displayed two rows of pearly white teeth.

"Selma," he repeated, taking her hand and brushing a brief kiss along her knuckles. "Nice to meet you. I'm Jonas Hinton."

She blinked. "Not Jonas Hinton, as in the new owner of the Carolina Panthers?"

Jonas's smile widened. "Guilty."

"Wow. It's a pleasure to meet you." Her gaze swept her surroundings. "You have a nice place. It's so big and...clean."

Solomon's gaze narrowed.

"What?" she asked.

At the sound of heels clicking across the floor, everyone turned.

Solomon sucked in a breath at the sight of Ophelia, resplendent in a fuchsia dress that hugged her voluptuous curves like a second layer of skin. His heart thumped wildly as a warm heat radiated throughout his body.

"Purple," Jonas said. He slid an arm around her small waist, and then leaned over to plant a kiss against her offered cheek. "Interesting choice."

An instant ache throbbed where Solomon's heart once resided. How in the hell was he going to get through this night?

Chapter 9

"You must be Selma." Ophelia stretched out her hand, while struggling to maintain a smile. "I'm pleased to meet you."

"Nice to finally meet you." A smile fluttered weakly on Selma's lips.

It took less than a nanosecond for Ophelia to size up Selma and note that although this married woman was attractive, Ophelia wouldn't have figured her to be Solomon's type—not that he had a type.

Releasing Selma's hand, Ophelia took note of the large diamond on the woman's finger. "Well, tonight's menu is Italian."

"Surprise, surprise," Solomon and Jonas chuckled in unison. Their gazes cut toward one another and all amusement faded.

"As you can tell, these two know Italian is my favorite," Ophelia informed Selma.

"And my chef is the master," Jonas added. "You'll love him."

"I, uh—" Selma glanced at Solomon "—don't normally like Italian, but, uh, sure, why not?"

Ophelia's smile tightened as her brain scrambled to figure out how to fix the situation. "I can get Raul to prepare something else, if you'd like?"

"No, no." Selma reached for her hands. "It's all right. I'm sure whatever you have prepared will be fine."

"Oh, you're engaged?" Jonas's attention lowered to the ring, and then to the band beneath it.

At his frown, Ophelia tugged him on the arm. "Honey, why don't we see if Raul can rustle something else up on short notice?"

Selma opened her mouth.

"It's not a problem," Ophelia said, cutting her off and still tugging on her fiancé. "Why don't you two just make yourself comfortable in the living room? We'll join you in a few minutes."

At their host and hostess's sudden disappearance, Solomon and Selma glanced at each other and burst out laughing.

"I guess she hasn't told him," Selma snickered, wiping at a stray tear.

"I think that's a safe assumption." He led her toward the first room adjacent to the foyer, and then leaned close to her ear. "Again, thanks for doing this for me."

"Yeah, the things I do for a free meal." She stopped in the center of the living room and took her time looking around. "Will you just check this place out? It's beautiful."

Solomon shrugged, unimpressed. "My place is just as nice."

"Maybe." She waltzed around and studied a few of

the knickknacks. "You know, I fail to see what you hope to accomplish by letting Ophelia think you're dating a married woman. Not that I'm not flattered."

"I told you. I choked—I wasn't thinking. Besides, she was just seconds away from pushing one of her girlfriends on me."

"You know, I don't get it. You're a very handsome man. Surely you don't need friends and a perverted uncle to find you a date. I mean, look at your office— that place is crawling with single women."

"Never mix business with pleasure. I learned that one from Marcel."

"The same Marcel that just married his secretary?"

Solomon cleared his throat. "Yeah, that one."

Selma rolled her eyes. "You need to just tell her how you feel. There, I said it."

"Again."

"Yes—again. Your problem is that you don't know how to take sound advice. It's no sweat off my nose if you allow the love of your life to walk out the door. I have my knight in shining armor waiting for me back home in New York."

"Yeah. Just wait until he hears that you're cheating on him with me," he joked.

"If anything, he'll have a good laugh." Her eyes rested on a picture of Jonas accepting an award of some kind. "I tell you what, this guy is pretty easy on the eyes. Those two will make some pretty babies, that's for sure."

Solomon's chest tightened.

"What is it?" Selma rushed to him.

"I-it's nothing." He massaged his chest.

Selma's maternal instincts kicked in, and she quickly placed a hand over his forehead to check his temperature.

"I'm fine, Selma." He removed her hand and then

placed his hands around her waist to physically move her away from him.

Ophelia and Jonas returned.

"Looks like we can't leave you two alone for a minute," Ophelia joked lightly after mistaking Solomon and Selma's pose.

Jonas also laughed, but its sound had lost all the genuineness it had held earlier. "Er, Raul can accommodate whatever you'd prefer—"

"No, no. Really. Italian will be fine. I appreciate you two going out of your way."

"It's really—"

"Italian it is," Solomon announced, irritated at how the conversation had bogged down over something as trivial as the dinner menu. Judging by how everyone's eyes shifted in his direction, his tone must have been a bit too harsh. "So, what does a person have to do to get a drink around here?" He laughed.

On cue, Benton appeared. "Can I get anything from the bar?"

"Scotch on the rocks," Solomon blurted.

Selma shook her head. "I'll have a Cosmopolitan."

Jonas and Ophelia also gave their drink orders, and then gestured for their guests to make themselves comfortable on the leather couches.

Solomon had never regretted anything more than accepting this dinner invitation. Other than the first eight minutes of being locked in the closet with Ophelia, he couldn't remember another time when he was actually nervous around her. Was this what the future held?

What was it going to be like in the coming years when he came by to see them—and their children? His thoughts stopped. There was another painful pinch in his chest.

Benton returned just in time with a tray of drinks.

However, the alcohol did little to loosen anyone up.

"So…I hear congratulations are in order?" Selma finally broke the silence. "Did Marcel and Diana's wedding inspire you?"

"You can say that," Ophelia smiled. "It was certainly a beautiful wedding."

"I'm sure it was. I saw some of the designs when Diana and her grandmother, Louisa, were planning it. I just hate that I had a sick kid on my hands and had to miss the whole event."

Ophelia took another sip of her drink. "You have children?"

"Oh, yes." Selma's smile brightened with pride. "I have three handsome boys—of course, they look a great deal like their father."

Solomon grabbed Selma's free hand and gave it a gentle squeeze.

Picking up on the hint, she clamped her mouth shut.

"Well, I'm sorry you missed it," Ophelia said softly. "I'm sure it was beautiful…and I'm sure yours will be just as lovely. When is the date?"

"November twelfth," Jonas boasted, giving his fiancée's waist an affectionate squeeze. "Then she'll be all mine." He kissed her.

Solomon rubbed at his chest.

Ophelia smiled and brushed the residue of her glossed lips from Jonas's. "Poor man just doesn't know what he's getting himself into." She chuckled. "Isn't that right, Solomon?"

"Apparently not."

"I think I'm up for the task," Jonas commented and managed to erase another inch between him and Ophelia.

"So." Ophelia smiled, but her desperation to ease the

tension was apparent. "How long have you two known each other?"

"Seven years," Selma answered.

At Ophelia's startled look, Solomon tossed back his drink and wished the burn had a stronger kick.

"That long?" Ophelia questioned.

"Well," Jonas perked up. His smile relaxed a bit more. "Good for you."

"Yeah," Ophelia added softly and took another sip of her drink.

Solomon knew her well enough to know she was pissed—more likely for having been kept in the dark than any spark of jealousy.

"And here I thought I knew you." Ophelia's lips sloped unevenly.

"I guess we all have our secrets," Solomon countered without missing a beat.

"Apparently some more than others," she jabbed, and then eased into another smile. "You'll have to forgive our sniping. I, for one, am happy Solomon has someone steady in his life—sort of. Maybe now I can stop worrying about him."

"Yes." Selma slid a hand down Solomon's leg until it settled on his knee. "That's my job now."

Ignoring his friend's boldness, Solomon forced a smile.

"Speaking of jobs," Jonas leaped at the opportunity to be a part of the conversation. "What do you do, Selma?"

"I'm an entertainment agent."

"Oh, so do you represent some of the acts at T & B?"

"Sure do. In fact, that's how Solomon and I met."

Music suddenly interrupted the stilted conversation,

and Selma scrambled for her purse. When she opened it, Solomon recognized the *Barney's* theme song.

"Hello." Pause. "Hey, Tommy, baby."

Solomon rolled his eyes.

"No, no. Mommy is not too busy right now." She covered her mouthpiece and mumbled an apology to her host and hostess.

Ophelia's gaze shifted to Solomon.

Miraculously, he held on to his smile.

"Yes, yes. He's right here."

Dread crept up Solomon's spine—and sure enough, Selma turned toward him and held out the phone.

"Tommy wants to talk to you."

Slack-jawed, Ophelia and Jonas watched him accept the phone.

"Hey, kid." At the sound of little Tommy's excited voice, Solomon dropped the pretense and enjoyed a hurried recap of the child's day. There was just something about his godson that never failed to put a smile on his face. "That's great," he said when the child finally managed to pause for a breath. "Yes, I'm going to keep my promise and take you and your brothers to Disney World."

Selma turned her smile toward the engaged couple. "The boys just love their Uncle Solomon."

"All right, all right. Here's your mom." He handed back the phone, still chuckling. When his gaze returned to Ophelia, his amusement faded.

Selma gave her love to her children and quickly disconnected the call. "Those are my babies," she bragged, and then glanced back at the stunned couple.

Ophelia and Jonas inhaled the rest of their drinks and requested Benton bring them each another.

"Sounds like you two have an interesting—arrangement."

Selma laughed. "I guess you can say that."

"Are you and your husband—separated?" Jonas asked with unmistakable hope in his voice.

"Oh, goodness no," Selma answered without glancing toward Solomon, and hence was oblivious to his hints to lie.

"Well, different strokes for different folks, I always say. We're not here to judge." Ophelia wondered if her words sounded as hollow to everyone else as they did to her. "Maybe I should go check with Raul and see how much longer dinner is going to be."

"I'll come with you," Jonas said.

Together they escaped the room as if the devil nipped at their heels.

Solomon's and Selma's gaze zoomed to each other, and another burst of laughter escaped their lips.

"You know, you're eventually going to have to tell her the truth," Selma said in between chuckles.

"Yeah, I know. But after tonight, I'm just starting to have a little fun."

Chapter 10

Jonas's harsh whisper brushed against his fiancée's ear. "Can you believe them?"

As a matter of fact, Ophelia couldn't. "It's none of our business," she reminded him.

"I know, but it's the casualness these two have toward their affair. I mean, what the hell is this world coming to? Hey, you don't think they're swingers, do you?"

She choked. "Oh, give me a break. They aren't the first people to have affairs."

"Maybe not, but most people try to keep something like that on the down low."

Crossing paths with Benton, Ophelia grabbed a new drink from his serving tray and tossed it back like a soldier who'd just cheated death.

In all the years she'd known Solomon, he'd never once hinted he was capable of living the type of dual life he was exhibiting tonight—and she didn't like it one bit.

"This just settles it for me. After we're married, you're not allowed to hang with this dude. Sex, drugs, and rock-n-roll. Humph. Not with my wife."

Ophelia stopped, and then slowly faced him. "What do you mean I'm not *allowed?* You're not my father."

"I never said I was your father. But that man——"

"Is my best friend."

"And marriage vows don't mean a damn thing to him. I don't trust him."

Her eyes lowered to thin slits. "You don't trust him, or me?"

Jonas's face twisted into a frown. "What are you talking about? I didn't say I didn't trust you."

"Then there's no problem."

His face darkened. "There most certainly is."

"How do you know her husband isn't completely okay with their relationship?"

"No man is okay with his wife sleeping around. Trust me."

"I've heard of open marriages."

"Open marriages were created for *men* to sleep around. Women turn a blind eye because the husband is a damn good provider. Unless it's a ménage à trois, men don't share."

"What?"

Jonas quickly tossed up his hands. "Hey, don't shoot the messenger."

"Excuse me?"

Jonas and Ophelia jumped, and then faced Solomon.

"You two might want to lower your voices. We can sort of hear you," he informed them.

Horrified, Ophelia gasped. "Oh, Sol. We didn't mean——"

"Forget it. Just try to lower your voices." He turned

with a smirk, but before he disappeared from sight, he turned again and met Jonas's stare. "And you don't have to worry about your girl around me—the ménage à trois isn't my thing—anymore."

Jonas glanced at Ophelia.

"He's kidding." Ophelia suppressed a grin. Her gaze lowered to watch Solomon's confident walk as he strolled back to the living room. An old sports injury caused his slight limp. She doubted anyone truly noticed, but she did. In fact, she remembered just about every story behind every scar, nick, or broken bone.

Solomon always had great stories—and she wondered what the real one was between him and Selma.

"Honey?"

"Huh? What?" She glanced at her fiancé and was stunned by the intensity of his stare. "What were you saying, sweetie?"

His shoulders slumped. "Nothing."

She wasn't buying it. She apparently had done something wrong. "Jonas—"

"We'd better get back in there," he said, offering his arm.

She abandoned her speech. What was the use? The night was a disaster. The whole purpose in inviting Solomon to dinner was to get two of the most important men in her life to at least tolerate one another.

Ophelia sighed, looped her arm through Jonas's, and brushed a kiss against his stiff lips.

Nothing.

No magic, no sparks, and definitely no butterflies.

When she pulled back, she beamed her best smile. It was becoming easier to hide her disappointment. And why not? It was such a small issue…or more like some crazy childhood fantasy about knights in shining armor, glass slippers, and bellies filled with butterflies. None of that stuff really happened. Well, it had happened once—twice—but that was long ago.

Arm in arm, Jonas led Ophelia back to the living room where everyone danced on eggshells. Ophelia tried her best not to like Selma, but the task was impossible. She was funny, smart, and kind. It was just this small issue of her being married with children that was throwing things off-kilter.

She cringed each time Solomon showed any type of affection toward Selma, and Ophelia hated how comfortable the two were around each other.

Dinner was finally served, not a moment too soon as far as Ophelia was concerned. She had already downed three drinks and was getting looser by the second.

"So where are you two going for your honeymoon?" Selma asked, once everyone had settled into the seats.

"We haven't really decided on a place," Jonas answered. "I'm a little partial to Mexico."

Ophelia and Solomon gazes crashed seconds before laughter filled the room.

Jonas and Selma's brows furrowed in curiosity.

"Sounds like we're missing something," Selma said.

"Let's just say that we have some pretty questionable memories about Mexico." Ophelia laughed.

"Questionable, hell," Solomon barked. "There's nothing wrong with my memory. You're the one who got trashed and thought you were a mermaid."

Another squeal of laughter peeled from Ophelia. "Oh, Lord."

Jonas's congenial smile slowly lowered to a thin, flat line. "Well, I can't wait to hear this one."

"No, no." Ophelia held up her hand. "Please, Sol. Don't say a word," she begged halfheartedly.

"But it's such a good story," Solomon said, dabbing his lips and carefully returning his napkin to his lap.

"Then I want to hear it, too," Selma said, smiling.

"Sorry, Ophelia." Solomon shrugged. "That makes three to one." He glanced at the other two. "Well, it was our high school senior trip to Cancun…"

Te Quiero

Chapter 11

The summer of '88 was perfect, and Cancun was the closest thing to heaven on earth, not just because of the white beaches and the clear blue ocean, but because the drinking age was eighteen.

Solomon, Ophelia, and Marcel checked into their room at the Omni Hotel and quickly prepared to create some great memories.

Marcel's plan was to simply stroll the beaches, hit the bars, and gather as many tenderonies as he could.

Ophelia had a list of activities—parasailing, deep-sea diving, and bungee jumping.

Solomon was just excited at the chance to finally put his four years of high-school Spanish to good use. Since he was also known for being the responsible one, he made sure he stopped his two best friends long enough to remind them to be careful with their money—to never take too much cash and always know where it is located. There were already rumors of other students losing their wallets.

"Yeah, yeah. We got it," Marcel said, rolling his eyes. "Man, try to relax. We're on vacation, remember?" He headed for the door.

"And don't drink the water," Solomon shouted toward his buddy's back.

"You worry too much," Ophelia said, withdrawing a yellow string bikini from her bag.

Solomon's brows arched. "You're not wearing that, are you?"

"After enduring a hundred crunches a day for the past three months, you're lucky I'm not running through this place butt naked."

Solomon swallowed a painful lump in his throat at the instant imagery. "The suit is fine."

"I'm glad you approve." She winked and rushed to the bathroom.

He waited for her, not sure why. Most likely, she was going to hang out with Tamara and Rachel. However, he never liked those two. He'd heard too many stories in the boy's locker room at school. The last thing he wanted was to have Ophelia's name added to the mix.

"So." He moved closer to the bathroom's door and crossed his arms. "What are you going to do first?"

"Oh, I don't know," she shouted back. "I hear a few people are going up to Fat Tuesday's. Maybe I'll go there. What about you?"

He shrugged and leaned against the door frame. He could easily catch up with Marcel and hang with the guys...but he didn't want to do that and be constantly worried about her. "I haven't decided."

"Well, you're more than welcome to hang with me."

When she opened the door, Solomon's eyes bulged

in surprise. Her body curved in all the right places and caused his most primal instincts to come alive.

"But if you're coming, you have to promise there won't be any blocking."

"What?" He had only caught the last word of her sentence.

"No blocking." She wrapped a sarong around her waist. "You and Marcel have a habit of chasing off guys who want to talk to me."

"Guys we know who are only after one thing."

"On this trip, I might just want one thing, too." She winked.

Solomon frowned. "What the hell does that mean?"

Ophelia locked her lips and pulled out her favorite pair of sandals.

"That settles it. I'm sticking with you."

"You're more than welcome to come," she said, checking her appearance in the closet mirror. "But I don't need a babysitter." Their gazes locked. "Catch my drift?"

He didn't trust himself to speak as he watched her sashay toward the door, but he followed as if in a trance.

It was one continuous party as the day morphed into night. Between bar hopping and tequila body shots, Solomon discovered it was a full-time job peeling men off his beautiful best friend.

Somehow they'd caught up to Marcel and his legion of women—not to say that Solomon didn't have his own choice of hotties, it was just none of them were Ophelia.

"Hey, man." Marcel draped an arm around his good buddy and shouted above the music. "Frank and them are talking about taking a booze cruise to Isla de las Mujeres. You want to tag along?"

"What the hell is a booze cruise?"

"Just what it sounds like—a boat with a lot of liquor. You game?"

Solomon glanced over his shoulder at Ophelia and her dance partner. He stepped forward, ready to fight if the guy didn't back off a couple of inches.

"Hey, hey." Marcel laid a restraining hand against Solomon's shoulders. "Let her have her fun."

Solomon's gaze swung in his direction and indicated with a slight nod for him to check their girl out.

A camera crew from something called *Girls Gone Wild* was headed in her direction.

Marcel blinked and headed toward her as well. "All right. We'll take her with us."

Minutes later, the three friends boarded a crowded yacht where the dancing and partying only intensified.

"You look like a great lay," a girl murmured against Solomon's ear.

"Excuse me?" He turned toward a stunning blonde.

"I said you look like a great lay." She danced her way closer. "I've never been with a black guy before."

Surely, Solomon misunderstood her. "Come again?"

"I just might." She winked and wiggled her assless rump against him.

Very carefully, Solomon detached himself from his crazy dance partner and tried his luck with a group of ebony babes doin' da butt.

Now he was having fun. After a while, Solomon's Ophelia radar kicked in and he glanced up to see her perched over a rail.

Was she sick?

He remembered Ophelia's low tolerance for alcohol, but he'd seen her drink like a fish for the better part of the day and night. Concerned about alcohol poisoning,

Solomon moved away from his nest of delectable women and headed toward Ophelia.

She wavered from side to side and occasionally dipped farther over the rail.

"Ophelia," he shouted, but he could barely hear himself over the loud music. He shouted again, and from the corner of his eye, he saw Marcel turn to see what was happening.

Ophelia held her head up, briefly, and then pitched forward and went over the railing.

"Ophelia!" Solomon and Marcel shouted in unison.

Solomon reached the spot where she had last stood and immediately climbed the rail and dove into the water without any thought to his own safety.

The ice-cold water was a shock to his system, but his arms and hands were already wading through the water in search of Ophelia.

He found her within seconds, and kicked his way up to the surface. As it turned out, their party boat had already docked at Isla de las Mujeres, and they were no more than a few yards from land.

"Ooh, look what my merman gave me," Ophelia cooed.

Solomon glanced at her and the small seashells she held up.

"What?" he panted.

"My merman. I'm a mermaid, and my merman just gave me these beautiful shells."

Oh, yeah, she was wasted.

Solomon swam them to shore, where a small crowd applauded his heroics and handed him another drink.

"Marcel, did I show you what my merman gave me?" Ophelia asked, slumping against him.

Marcel laughed as he caught her, and Solomon just rolled his eyes.

It was hours before the three friends returned to the hotel room. Marcel was barely standing, and Solomon was left to carry a knocked-out Ophelia into the room. He prayed the whole week wasn't going to be like this. He had a sneaking suspicion that, indeed, it would. There were two beds in the room, and one cot. Of course, if Ophelia's parents ever found out about their sleeping arrangements, there would undoubtedly be hell to pay. Marcel was supposed to take the cot, but he wasn't in the room a full minute before he'd passed out on one of the beds.

Sighing, Solomon carried Ophelia to the last available bed. As he laid her down, a faint whisper fell from her lips. "Te quiero."

He tensed and then stared at her sleeping form. "What did you say?" He waited for what seemed like forever, and just when he thought that she had fallen asleep, her eyes fluttered open.

A lazy smile eased across her lips as she lifted her hand and gently caressed the side of his face. "You always take such good care of me," she whispered.

"I do what I can." He kissed her hand. "You better get some sleep."

Her smile widened briefly and then her eyelids slowly lowered. "Te quiero."

Solomon leaned forward and brushed a paternal kiss against her forehead. "Yeah, I love you, too."

Chapter 12

"No one can say that you don't have balls," Selma snickered as she eased into the passenger seat of Solomon's black Hummer. "Why in the hell did you tell the man his fiancée kept murmuring she loved you in her sleep?"

"I just said what happened." Solomon slammed her door shut. He glided to the driver's side, failing to see what was the big deal. When he finally opened his door, he caught the last few notes of Selma's amused laughter.

"I thought the man was going to come out of his seat and choke the living daylights out of you," she admitted.

"It wasn't that serious." He started the vehicle.

"Uh-uh. And the Pope isn't Catholic."

Solomon shook his head and pulled out of the parking garage. In retrospect, the dinner table had gone awfully quiet after his short stroll down memory lane.

"If Jonas is insecure about me and Ophelia's relationship, that's his problem, not mine."

"It'll be your problem if he prohibits Ophelia from seeing you."

"What?" Solomon glanced over at her. "He can't do that. Besides, Ophelia wouldn't agree to it. We've been best friends since—"

"If nothing, marriage is a list of compromises. Sure, you're her best friend, but if the love of her life is uncomfortable with you being in the picture, then what do you think she's going to do?"

"The love of her life?"

"She agreed to marry him, didn't she?"

Solomon held his tongue.

"Look, as your friend, I'm just telling you like it is," Selma continued. "If Marty had a problem with our relationship, I would do what's in my power to get you two to get along. If that didn't work, then I'm sorry, but I'd have to cut you loose. Ace trumps king. It's as simple as that."

He hated to admit it, but Selma made sense. However, he had a hard time accepting Jonas as the love of Ophelia's life. His mind replayed the evening's events. Ophelia had spent most of the time nestled in Jonas's arms and grinning cheekily at the man's boastful stories of big business deals.

Money was a big deal to Mr. Hinton. How he made it, how much he saved, and how much he flaunted it. True, Solomon was no pauper, but he was no braggart either.

"Love of her life, humph."

"What did you say?"

His gaze slid to Selma. He had forgotten she was in the car. "Nothing."

Selma shook her head. "Well, I guess it could've been

worse. The story didn't end with you two having sex. That would have been a nightmare."

Solomon fell silent as he concentrated on the road.

"You two never had sex together," Selma asked with suspicion dripping from her tone. "Right?"

He didn't respond.

"Solomon?"

Jonas was furious. He wanted to throw or hit something—or rather someone—Solomon. Now more than ever, he was convinced that there was more to Solomon and Ophelia's relationship than either was letting on.

Te quiero. He glanced over at his fiancée as she headed toward her separate bedroom. He glared at the fuchsia dress she'd chosen to wear. *Solomon always said I looked good in this color.*

"I'm going out for a drive," he announced.

"What?" Ophelia faced him and then glanced down at her watch. "But it's nearly midnight."

"I need some air." He stormed toward the door.

"Wait. I'll go with you," she offered.

"I'd rather you didn't." He jerked open the door, but felt her hand land on his shoulder before he cleared the threshold. Closing his eyes, he refused to turn around.

"I know what you're thinking," she said. "And you're wrong."

"Am I?" A pathetic rumble of laughter shook his tall frame. "The thing I'm trying to figure out is if you're lying to me or to yourself."

"Solomon is just a friend. He has always been *just* a friend."

"Te quiero."

Ophelia sighed. "I was eighteen, drunk—"

"You love him."

"Of course I love him. I love Marcel, too. We've known each other for years."

Jonas almost wavered, and then forced himself to ask the question most prominent in his mind. "And if you had to choose between me or him?"

"Is that supposed to be some kind of ultimatum?"

"And if it was?"

The instant silence was like a knife through the heart, and after a few long, drawn-out seconds, he jerked his shoulder from her grasp.

"Jonas," she called weakly.

He didn't turn around.

Ophelia watched him go and slumped wearily against the door's archway. It was the perfect ending to a horrible night, and it was all Solomon's fault.

She huffed out an annoyed breath and went back inside the condominium.

Benton appeared out of the blue. "Is there anything else I can get you this evening, ma'am?"

"No." She smiled. "That will be all for the night. Thank you."

Benton bowed and exited as quickly as he'd appeared.

And just like that she was alone—alone with her thoughts and her roller-coaster emotions. Just what the hell was she doing? Did she even have a clue?

Two weeks ago she was excited—no, she was ecstatic at Jonas's spontaneous proposal. And now?

Ophelia closed her eyes. Maybe she was just upset. Rightfully so, with Jonas bolting without even attempting to resolve the issue like two rational adults. "I'm going for a drive. Humph. He's not going to keep pulling that stunt." She stormed toward her bedroom and then slammed the door behind her.

The loud bang at least gave her some small measure of satisfaction—so she did it again.

She sucked in a deep breath and then did something she hadn't done in years: she started crying. Why, exactly, she wasn't sure. However, once the dam broke, there was no stopping it.

Blurry eyed, she headed toward the bathroom and snatched sheets of Kleenex out of a small, pink box in a sad attempt to dry her tears, but they kept coming—pouring, actually.

"Damn him," she finally mumbled and then added, "Damn them both."

Peeling out of her clothes, she submerged herself beneath a stream of steaming hot water until her tears abated. However, her emotions continued to go all over the map.

Shutting off the shower, Ophelia grabbed the nearest towel. Instead of drying off, she wrapped the plush towel around her wet body and slinked off to her bedroom. Vaguely, she wondered if Jonas had returned, but she didn't go check.

She refused to be forced to choose between him and Solomon.

But what if you have to?

Ophelia closed her eyes and lay across the bed. This was her and Jonas's first disagreement, she realized. They shouldn't go to bed angry. Hadn't her mother taught her that advice on marriage?

You're not married yet.

She sighed and reached for one of the bed pillows. It was a lousy substitute for comfort, but the other option, calling her best friend, was out of the question as well.

She heard a slam and sat up in bed.

Jonas had returned home.

Seconds stretched into minutes while Ophelia strained to listen for his footsteps. When she finally heard them in the hallway, she drew and held her breath.

Should she go to him, wait for him, or ignore him?

Problem was, she wanted to do all those things as well as scream at him, hit him, and break off their engagement. Her heart squeezed. Where had that last thought come from?

The footsteps grew louder.

She needed to make a decision, but she couldn't. She was rooted to the edge of the bed, while her heart hammered against her rib cage.

The footsteps stopped at her door. Any second he would knock, and she would have to reach a decision.

While waiting for his soft rap, her lungs threatened to explode. Yet, she refused to release the air locked in them.

The silence was deafening, the wait excruciating. But the knock never came. Instead, she listened as he walked away.

The instant stab of disappointment surprised her, as well as the wave of fresh tears. Ophelia fell back against the bed, submerged in misery and confusion. Another door slammed at the other end of the hall, and silent tears slowly leaked from her eyes.

She had made her decision.

Solomon groaned at the sound of a ringing phone. He couldn't imagine who was calling—he peeked at the glowing red numbers on his clock—at three in the morning. Briefly, he wavered between answering and ignoring the damn thing, but finally decided to pick up.

"This better be important," he growled with his eyelids at half-mast.

"Sol?" came Ophelia's unmistakable voice.

He was instantly alert. His ears became attuned to her sniffles and upset tone. "What's wrong, Ophelia?"

When she didn't readily answer, Solomon's mind rushed through a long list of things her jerk of a fiancé could've done. His temper escalated as he jumped out of bed and headed toward his closet.

"I'm coming over," he declared.

"No," she croaked. "I don't need you to come over." More sniffles.

His footsteps slowed while his hand tightened on the receiver. "Then tell me what's wrong?"

He listened to her draw a long, shaky breath. "I don't know if I can do this."

His shoulders relaxed as he sighed in relief. She wasn't going to marry this dude after all. "It's okay. You don't have to do anything that you don't want to."

"I wish that were true," she answered shakily. "But Sol…I can't see you anymore."

Solomon froze, unable to comprehend what he'd just heard.

"I'm sorry, but I have to do this if I'm going to make this work with Jonas. And I *do* want to make this work."

"Ophelia—"

"Please, Sol. Try to understand. He's important to me."

"More important than I am?" he thundered into the receiver. "You can just throw everything we've been through together out the window—just like that?"

"This isn't easy for me."

"You could've fooled me."

"Sol—"

"You've known this jerk for four months, and me for more than half your life."

"Sol—"

"Who has always been there for you—been through boyfriends, and bailed you out of jail after one silly college protest after another?"

"This isn't about any of that. I love Jonas."

Solomon's rage only multiplied at hearing those words. "Yeah, well, I love you, too, and look where the hell that's gotten me."

She was crying harder now, and he waited, desperately wanting her to respond to what he'd just confessed.

"I'm marrying Jonas," she sobbed. "I'm sorry, Sol."

"Ophelia."

She disconnected the call.

"Ophelia," he shouted and waited. After a few seconds, a recording came on the line, instructing him how to make a call. He hung up and tried to call Ophelia back. She didn't answer her cell phone. Instead of leaving a message, he hurled the cordless phone across the room.

A mirror exploded. He stood immobile while he listened to shattered glass crash against the wooden floor. It was the perfect metaphor for what was happening to his heart.

Chapter 13

Ophelia tucked her feet beneath her on the window seat and clutched her cell phone against her heart. The call was supposed to solve her problems. Now it felt as if she'd just made everything worse.

Well, I love you, too, and look where the hell that's gotten me.

She shook her head and tried to erase his voice. There was no point in trying to read anything more into his words. Solomon had undoubtedly meant that he loved her as a friend—just as she did him. But...

Ophelia drew another deep breath and winced at the pain suddenly throbbing around her heart. She set the phone down beside her and rubbed her chest while she wondered what life would be like without Solomon.

Her hand stilled while she wrapped her brain around that notion. Hell, she could barely remember a time when she didn't know Solomon. Whether he was the catcher signaling for a fastball or the teammate guarding her while she tried her best to do a slam dunk.

He was always there.

Memories, too many to count, clamored to the surface: ten minutes in heaven, skinny-dipping in old man Homer's private lake, Cancun, and...

Undeniable warmth rushed across her body, and a maddening flutter of butterflies swarmed her insides. Solomon had been more than the first boy to kiss her, or the first boy to knock Billy Cohn's block off for calling her chicken legs. Solomon was the man she chose—and it was a choice—to give her most precious gift...

Just Between Us

Chapter 14

It was a dark and rainy night on October 12, 1991, and Ophelia had never been more nervous in her life. After all, it was a big and important night. It was her twenty-first birthday, and she was going to seduce her best friend—or try, anyway.

Being a junior at Spelman College, Ophelia was more than a little disappointed that she was still a big "V." Although there wasn't a shortage of willing and able men to do the honors, Ophelia had trouble finding the *right* man for the job.

The last thing she wanted to do was to give some dumb Atlanta U. jock bragging rights or become just another notch on some wannabe playa's bedpost.

Ophelia wanted her first time to be special. She wanted it to be with a man who was gentle and who would take his time. Unfortunately, in the three years she'd been in college, she had yet to meet the guy that fit the bill.

And her patience had come to an end.

Now, she'd had a few close calls—caught-up-in-the-moment kind of things—but the guy would inevitably say something rude, crass, or downright stupid to bring things to a screeching halt.

All of that would end tonight.

In retrospect, she didn't know why she hadn't thought of Solomon before. He was the ultimate kind and patient man whom she was more than a little comfortable around. She knew he'd dated around, but Solomon wasn't the kiss-and-tell type.

Once the thought of Solomon being the solution to her problems popped into her head, she couldn't easily let go of it. She made a list of props and cons, called Dionne Warwick's Psychic Friends Network, and even visited a palm reader during her trip to New Orleans during Mardi Gras: Solomon was perfect.

The last decision to make was to pin down an actual date. What better night than on her birthday?

She glanced around the tiny apartment at the multitudes of scented candles. There were so many, in fact, it sort of resembled a holy shrine. On the coffee table sat a chilled bottle of champagne, a bowl of strawberries, and a canister of whipped cream.

As for her attire, she had decided on a lacy fuchsia teddy and matching silk robe. However, after she had spent the last two hours primping, she finally wondered what she was going to do if Solomon said no.

Ophelia's stomach twisted into a huge knot. In that instant, she realized what an incredible risk she was taking and what was at stake. Sex changed people. She wasn't so naive to think otherwise.

What if, afterward, she fell for Solomon? It wasn't totally out of the question. She had seen some oddly paired couples around campus. She thought about it. Solomon wouldn't be a bad boyfriend—but what if it didn't work out? Could they go back to being best friends?

She doubted it.

Most likely if it didn't work out, she could kiss their friendship goodbye. Ophelia walked over to the couch and eased down into its plush cushions. Suddenly the list of cons grew by leaps and bounds.

"What the hell was I thinking?" she mumbled under her breath. She jumped to her feet and rushed to the phone near the coat closet.

The doorbell rang.

The phone receiver seemed glued to her hand. Even after the second ring, she couldn't move. Maybe if she didn't answer, he would just go away.

Another ring blended with a quick rap against the door.

A loud insistent tone blared from the phone. She quickly hung it up and prayed that it hadn't been loud enough for Solomon to hear.

Everything was silent for a moment, and then she heard a key slide into the lock. She had forgotten he had a key.

Fleeing popped into her mind, but before she could take a step, the door opened.

"Who in the hell died?" Solomon's gruff baritone filled the apartment. "This place looks like a mortuary." He stepped inside and slowly closed the door. In his hand, he carried a small gold box.

Before she could say anything, his curious gaze found her standing by the closet.

Neither spoke while his gaze slid down her body.

Over the years, Solomon had seen her in less—but he had never looked at her like this before. His eyes warmed and then darkened slightly.

"Did I come at bad time?" he asked.

Suddenly English was a foreign language, and Ophelia couldn't manage to utter a sound, let alone a full sentence.

"I thought we were hanging out tonight, but, uh…" He glanced around again. "I take it you had a change of plans?"

Still nothing.

Solomon's gaze traveled over her again before he seemed to force himself out of his trance. "I better come back another time." He turned toward the door and nearly tripped over air.

When she laughed, Solomon flashed her an embarrassed smile. "I guess I better go." His hand landed on the doorknob.

This was it, she realized: now or never.

Solomon opened the door and stepped forward. He was going to leave.

She was going to let him.

He was leaving.

She remained silent.

He was going…going…

"Wait." Ophelia's heart instantly leaped into her throat.

The silence seemed to go on forever before Solomon's head poked around the door.

"Uh." She cleared her throat. "Don't go. I haven't made any other plans."

His face scrunched in confusion, but he made no move to reenter the apartment.

"Really," she said and added a shaky smile, and then

dropped it when she felt like a cheap car dealer pushing a Yugo on a Mercedes man.

When he'd at last ascertained that she was being serious, Solomon slowly crept back inside and closed the door. "Were you in the middle of changing or something?"

Forcing an air of confidence she didn't feel, Ophelia took her first steps toward him. "Is that for me?" she asked, purposely ignoring his question.

He glanced down at the box and then lifted it toward her. "Happy twenty-first."

Smiling, she reached for the neatly wrapped package and made sure she stood close enough for Solomon to catch the soft fragrance of her perfume. She took her time opening the gift, but her confidence waned when Solomon stepped back.

What if she made a fool of herself? Her hands trembled while they fumbled with the box.

"If you don't like it, I can take it back," Solomon said before she opened the jeweler's velvet box.

"Don't be silly, I'm sure whatever it is, I'm going to—" She gasped. Her eyes roamed, and then misted at the sight of a beautiful diamond tennis bracelet, the same bracelet she had been ogling at Opulence jewelry store for the past year. "Oh, Sol. It's beautiful." She moved past him to lean against the arm of the couch.

"May I?"

Solomon's warm breath rushed against the shell of her ear and caused a quick shiver to course through her body. She glanced up at him while he removed the bracelet from its box. She found herself mesmerized by every curve and line of his face. Though he wasn't what most women called a pretty boy, he was indeed handsome.

When Ophelia felt Solomon loop the bracelet around her wrist, she lowered her gaze to marvel at the spectacular gift. It was simply beautiful, but... "Sol, I can't accept this."

"Why not?"

"For one thing, you can't afford something like this. This had to cost a fortune." She hiked her brows in suspicion. "It is real?"

Solomon rolled his eyes. "Now what kind of question is that?"

"A good question."

"Hey, it's not the price that matters, but the thought behind it."

Ophelia relaxed. Of course it wasn't real. Where on earth would Solomon get ten grand to buy the tennis bracelet at Opulence? She glanced at her wrist again and had to admit that she was impressed with this knockoff. "You're right. It's the thought that counts."

A broad smile hugged his lips, a nice pair of juicy—

"Shouldn't you finish getting dressed?" he asked, moving to take a seat on the couch.

"What?" She blinked, out of her trance.

"Aren't you going to get dressed, or do you plan on going out in that? Not that I mind, I've always thought you looked good in that color."

She glanced down at herself and then tugged at her robe when she realized how close she was to spilling out of the top of her teddy. She joined him on the couch, and her gaze quickly slithered over to him.

He gave a sly smile. "I didn't see anything."

She smiled back and then forced the next sentence out of her mouth. "I was hoping that we could stay in."

"But I thought you had Prince tickets?"

She sucked in a breath, totally prepared to deliver

the lie she'd practiced earlier. But at the last minute, she decided to go with the truth. "I lied."

The two words seemed to hang in the air between them for an eternity before Solomon spoke.

"Why?"

She hesitated.

"I mean if you just wanted to hang out and have a Blockbuster night, we could've invited Marcel. He was sort of pissed you didn't at least get three tickets tonight." He glanced at his watch. "We can probably page him and see if he wants to come over. I'm sure he wants to spend time with you on you birthday." He started to get up.

Ophelia placed a restraining hand against his leg.

Solomon's frown returned. "What's the matter? Don't you—"

She placed her finger against his lips to silence him. After drawing a shaky breath, she boldly met her best friend's curious stare. "I don't want Marcel to come over. I don't want to go out. And I'm not changing clothes."

Ophelia waited while her words and her meaning sank in. When she was sure it had, she slowly removed her finger from his lips. "Sol, I have a big favor to ask you."

He didn't respond.

"And please, whatever you do, don't laugh at this. Okay?"

Still silent, he nodded.

Ophelia drew another deep breath. "Sol, for my twenty-first birthday, I want you to be my first. Will you make love to me?"

Chapter 15

Solomon stared at Ophelia, afraid to ask her to repeat the question. It wasn't until after the silence had stretched to its capacity that he realized she was waiting for an answer.

He coughed, cleared his throat, and then coughed some more. Was this some kind of a joke? Were Marcel and their frat brothers going to jump out at any moment with a camcorder? "Uh, what—?"

"Look, you don't have to if you don't want to," Ophelia said. Her pretty cheeks darkened. "I just thought that...." She released a long sigh. "Hell, I don't know what I thought."

Solomon's gaze darted, yet again, to the candles, champagne, and strawberries. "Seems you went to an awful lot of trouble," was all he could think to say.

She tied the belt on her robe. "Well, I sort of wanted the night to be...special."

It would have been hard to ignore the note of disappointment in her voice. She was serious.

"Thanks for not laughing at me," Ophelia added, avoiding his gaze.

He drew a deep breath in an attempt to calm his building excitement. "May I ask you something?"

She shrugged, while still having trouble landing her gaze. "Sure."

"Why me?"

"There're lots of reasons," she said simply.

"Name one."

She looked at him. Her eyes glossed with unshed tears. "Because you're my best friend. You know me better than anyone. I trust you to be kind, gentle, and patient with me. I *want* to do this with you."

A long silence stretched between them before Solomon leaned forward. Every muscle in his body was tight with anticipation. Sure, they'd kissed each other often, but those were mere pecks on the cheek or light brushes against her forehead. This was different.

The moment their lips connected, Solomon melted at the sound of her sigh and the blaze of an inferno roaring within him. This was no awkward adolescent kiss. This was a strange and intoxicating combination of hunger, passion, and undeniable longing.

His longing.

Solomon pressed closer, already addicted to the faint taste of strawberries on her lips. Gently, Ophelia's soft hands cupped the sides of his face and pulled him even closer to her scantily clad body. He followed her lead and then stopped when she gasped. His solid erection brushed against her leg, and her gaze lowered to view its visible outline against his pants.

He knew what was racing through her mind. The last

time they'd seen each other naked was years ago when they had gone skinny-dipping, and frankly, he'd grown considerably over the years.

Waiting for her gaze to return to his face, Solomon was suddenly aware that this intimate moment could come to a screeching halt. What would he do if it did?

Time stood still while his erection only hardened and his heart nearly hammered its way out of his chest. At long last, her beautiful golden eyes traveled upward to lock gazes.

"I just remembered another reason why I chose you," she said huskily.

Solomon came to her with a groan, crashing their lips in another meaningful and needy kiss. However, it was the strangest thing—the more he drank from her sweet mouth, the thirstier he became. That didn't make sense.

A once-nervous Ophelia floated languidly on heaven's lofty clouds. She remembered having this same experience years before, but after so much time had passed, she'd convinced herself she'd imagined the whole thing. Everything tingled, tickled, or fluttered wonderfully, and he had yet to remove a single article of clothing.

Yet fear had a way of wheedling itself into any situation. She worried whether her experienced best friend would be turned off by her skills—or lack thereof—in the bedroom. At first, she tried to push the thought aside, but the question kept resurfacing.

She tore her lips away, much to the relief of her oxygen-deprived lungs, and sucked in a long, shaky breath.

"Is something wrong?" Solomon panted.

"Maybe we should talk."

He slumped forward with unmistakable disappointment.

"Please," she added. "Just for a minute."

He closed his eyes, nodded, and drew in a deep breath before he pushed himself off of her.

Instantly, her body cried out in protest at the absence of his body heat. She took it as a signal to make her speech short and sweet.

"I'm nervous, I'm new at this, and I hope you won't be disappointed." There, she'd said it. She reached for him again and pulled him back.

"That's it?" he asked.

She heard the laughter in his voice and she smiled. "Not unless you have something else you want to add."

"Hell, no." Solomon peeled off his dark turtleneck with a quick *whoosh* before he reclaimed his position above her.

Catching only a glimpse of his bare, smooth chest was enough to accelerate Ophelia's wild heartbeat, but the joy of feeling it beneath her hands was immeasurable. While she absorbed everything he was willing to give, she playfully and tenderly slid her fingers over every inch of his chest and back. The many corded muscles that flexed and tightened intrigued her.

When she finished the exploration, her fingers lowered to the waist of his pants. Caught up in what she was feeling, she didn't think to be surprised by her bold moves.

Solomon pulled away, and she was left to stare at him in bewilderment.

"Are you sure you've never done this before?"

Stuck between embarrassment and flattery, she chuckled. "Am I doing something you like?"

"You're doing everything I like." He smiled and gave

her a wink. "But maybe we should do this the right way." He stood up.

Ophelia frowned. "Are we doing something wrong?" She watched him cross the room to her old stereo in the corner.

"No. I just think we should make the night as special as we can." Once he selected and inserted a CD, the smooth, hot tunes from Jodeci filled the room.

She didn't know what to say, but she appreciated him caring so much.

He approached the couch again and held out his hand. "Maybe we should start off with a little dancing."

She glanced up at him. He had a wonderful smile. She thought about that while sliding her hand into his. Ophelia stood and glided easily into his arms, where once again his bare chest brushed against the thin, lacy material of her teddy and his ever-present hard erection pressed against other parts. Weak-kneed by just the thoughts of things to come, she didn't know how she managed to sway in time with the music.

"Strawberries and champagne?" Solomon asked.

"And whipped cream," she added, and then blanched in embarrassment.

Solomon chuckled. "No, let's not forget that."

Certain that her face was turning every shade of red, Ophelia buried her head against his chest, but soon found that she loved the sound of his steady heartbeat. By the second track of the CD, she was completely relaxed and at ease. She didn't give it a thought when he tilted up her chin and once again swept her mind away with another kiss.

Time stood still, the earth moved, her stomach filled with thousands of butterflies—every flowery prose she'd ever read in a romance novel was actually happening to her, and she couldn't be more pleased.

Solomon gently slid off her silk robe and then took his time lowering the spaghetti straps from her shoulders. His dear best friend had no idea how long he'd dreamed of this night, and he was going to make sure they savored every moment.

He pulled her teddy down until it reached her waist and then gently cupped her full breasts. He devoured her soft gasp and absolutely fell in love with the feel of her hard nipples in the palm of his hand. He played with them until they grew even harder.

He needed a bed. He had no intention of taking her right there on the floor or even on the small contraption she and her roommate called a couch. With his mind made up, he broke their kiss, swept her half-nude body up into his arms, and carried her toward her bedroom.

However, when he pushed open the door, he was surprised to find more candlelight, chilled champagne, strawberries...and whipped cream awaited him.

"I see you put some thought into this."

Ophelia giggled. "A little." She smiled up at his handsome face, pleased that everything was going so well.

His gaze darkened with desire, and it literally stole her breath. In the next moment, she was being lowered onto the bed. She forgot her breasts were still exposed, but when Solomon's gaze deserted hers, she was suddenly embarrassed and crossed her arms to cover herself.

His smile warmed. "Don't do that. You're beautiful." Gently, he pulled her hands away.

Laying still, she watched as he reached for her, even quivered when his finger brushed against her hard nipples. An ache seemed to resonate from her very soul while she waited for more.

It wasn't a long wait.

Solomon leaned down and kissed her, a deep, devouring kiss that left them both breathless. During that time he also managed to slide the lacy lingerie from her body and reveal a small nest of curls between her legs.

No doubt about it: Ophelia Missler was all grown up.

"What about you?" she asked softly. "Can I see you?"

He shot to his feet and reached to unbutton his pants when she stopped him.

"Can I do it?" Her hands replaced his and, although shaky, unbuttoned his pants.

He watched and waited. The pants fell off easily enough, but the hesitation came once she reached the boxers.

"Hey." Solomon brushed her hands away. "We don't have to do this if you don't want to." He said the words and meant them, but predicted years of therapy if she did change her mind.

"No. I want to do this," she said in an adorable pout, while her hands returned to his boxers and slid them off.

Ophelia's eyes widened and twinkled in the candlelight. "You're beautiful, too," she whispered.

They reached for each other in the same moment. Her arms wrapped around his neck as he eased her gently onto her back. Their lips locked, their hands explored, and the room was filled with sighs and moans.

The heat of his arousal, pressed so intimately against her, overwhelmed and thrilled her. Through it all, he remained surprisingly gentle. Yes, she'd made the right choice.

Her wild response to him was overwhelming, and all plans of patience and restraint were quickly being tossed out the window. Finally, he dragged his mouth away to delve and taste the fragrant valley between her breasts. However, it wasn't long before he drew a hard tan nipple into his mouth. As a mere mortal, this was his first taste of heaven, and as long as this night never ended, he couldn't care less if he never returned to earth.

Solomon reveled in the feel of her soft breasts rubbing against his face. While he took his time switching from one taut bud to the other, his hand stroked a path downward. Gently, he caressed her inner thighs, occasionally brushing the downy V between her legs.

Ophelia moaned at the sweet torture and even tried to thrust her hips toward his roaming hand. However, each time his strong fingers drew near, they ignored her open invitation and nearly made her mad with longing.

"Sol?" she panted.

"Hmm?" He continued his slow suckling.

"Please—I can't take much more…"

On cue, Solomon dipped two fingers into her warm, slick passage.

She almost came off the bed as tremors of raw pleasure rocketed throughout her body. Thinking was impossible, breathing was nearly so, but ecstasy consumed her. The smooth, long strokes of his fingers were like nothing she had ever experienced, and something she didn't want to end.

Ophelia's mouth moved, but she was clueless as to what she was saying. Her hips picked up the pace, matching his hand stroke for stroke.

Solomon's desire to taste all of her overpowered him, and his mouth soon followed the trail his hand had taken. He rained small kisses down the valley between her breasts, the flat plane of her stomach, and then finally the lips of her femininity.

"Sol…"

His mouth covered the very heat of her, and his tongue delivered pleasure so intense tears instantly sprang to her eyes. She lowered her hands to caress the sides of his face while she continued to rotate her hips at the same languid pace as his divine tongue.

Something wonderful was building inside of her—a bliss so sweet her entire body tensed in preparation. But as this burgeoning feeling drew closer, she suddenly was trying to back away.

Solomon would have none of that. His hands locked onto her hips, holding her in place.

Her caresses stopped, and she tried to push him away. Frantic, she glanced down at him, but their gazes locked, and then she could do little more than watch his mouth's loving worship.

Her voice raced up the musical scale, and when her first orgasm hit, they discovered that she was indeed a soprano.

Satisfied with her reaction, Solomon crawled up the bed to lie beside her, his hands stroking her body. "Since I wasn't planning anything like this tonight, I don't have a condom on me. You didn't happen to remember—"

"Oh." She sat up in bed. "I bought a box. They're in the bathroom." Ophelia went to get up, but Solomon restrained her.

"I'll get them," he said, brushed a kiss against her temple, rushed out of the room, and bounded across the hall to the bathroom. He found the box of Trojans rather easily, and out of consideration took a few minutes to wash his face and swish a Dixie cup of Listerine. After that, he headed back toward Ophelia's bedroom.

A startled gasp caught his attention, and he was

stunned when he turned toward Ophelia's roommate, Kailua.

Her eyes traveled down the length of him and froze at the sight of his erection.

"Sorry," he said with a smile and strolled back to Ophelia's room. Closing the door, he emitted a small chuckle.

"What's so funny?" Ophelia asked.

Solomon eased back onto the bed. "I think I just surprised your roommate."

"She's home?" Ophelia sat up. "She's not supposed to be back until tomorrow." Ophelia hopped off the bed.

Solomon, frightened their time together was over, quickly reached for her. "Wait. Where are you going?"

"To see what she's doing here."

"Does it matter?" he asked, pressing her back down onto the bed. "She has her own room. I'm just getting started with you," he said, and sealed his lips against hers in another tantalizing kiss.

She relaxed and eased back onto the bed—ready for round two.

Chapter 16

Ophelia wanted to learn everything Solomon could teach. Yet, she didn't quite understand how he was able to send her from one heavenly plateau to another. First it was his kisses, his hands, and then his talented tongue. And now with his heavy sex pressed against the apex of her womanhood, she was positively quaking for what would come next.

She heard the small rip of the condom packet and watched him through the mesh of her lowered lashes as he sheathed his hard member with the lubricated latex. This was actually going to happen, she realized. It was her last chance to back out.

She almost laughed at the thought. There was no way in the world she was going to back out of this now. She had waited too long and come too far.

"Are you sure you want to do this?"

Solomon's passion-filled baritone forced her gaze to

leap up and meet his boldly. "Shut up and kiss me," she ordered with a lazy smile.

He did just that. He liked her boldness and even liked the little moans she made, too, when he drew her closer. Gently, he separated her thighs with one of his own, and then braced his weight on his elbows so that his body covered hers.

Solomon worried about the initial pain she would feel, and then worried whether his length and size would be too much for a virgin. But worrying didn't mean he was backing out.

There was no way in hell he was doing that.

However, if he didn't enter her soon, he was going to go insane. He distracted her with kisses and forced her to hold still by holding the sides of her hips. He hesitated at her soft entry, and then eased in slowly.

Ophelia gasped; but when he continued to sink deeper, she cried out. "Stop, stop. Wait, wait." She needed to catch her breath, yet couldn't.

"Shh, shh. Don't move," Solomon instructed. "Just relax and let your body adjust."

Tears leaked from her eyes as she followed his instructions. To her amazement, the pain was already ebbing away.

Solomon kissed the tracks of her tears. "Tell me again if you truly want me to stop."

Her eyes met his, and she was mesmerized by their intensity and felt that, somehow, she was drowning in their depths.

"Do you want me to stop?"

Slowly, she shook her head.

"I want to hear you say it," he whispered.

"No," she answered in the same silky tone. "I don't want you to stop," she added to make sure that she was clear. When he moved inside her, the pain blended with something sweet—something wonderful.

Solomon drew a few deep breaths in order to maintain his control. She was so sinfully tight and warm that he feared he would explode prematurely. Soon, soft lyrical moans tumbled from her lips, and still he was able to maintain a sliver of control.

"Don't stop, Sol. Don't ever stop," she panted.

During his slow, measured strokes, Solomon buried his face in the crook of her neck and groaned at the exquisite feel of her.

A mindless Ophelia thrashed restlessly. How delicious it was that he filled her completely, but she no longer wanted this patient gentleness. Her body needed—demanded—more. She dug her nails into his soft skin and locked her legs tightly around his hips, which forced him to sink even deeper. More tears slid from the corners of her eyes as that wondrous feeling from the core of her soul began to spread.

Solomon's smooth strokes morphed into deep thrusts. And, Lord, he'd never felt anything this wonderful in all his life. The bed creaked and the headboard banged against the wall. But, frankly, neither cared if the whole damn thing broke, it wasn't going to stop this groove.

After a long while, a fine sheen of sweat covered them, and the satin sheet clung to them as well.

While Solomon's hips hammered away, he reached in between their joined bodies and rubbed the soft bud between her legs.

Her thrashes intensified until Ophelia finally surrendered to her second orgasm, which hit her with the force of an atomic blast. She clung to Solomon in fear that she would die from the shockwaves quaking throughout her body.

However, it was those tiny tremors that finally pitched Solomon over the edge. His guttural moans were not without a level of spirituality. His shudder of release was both violent and sweet. His love deepened for this magnificent woman, and he intended to spend the entire night showing her just how much.

When the final quiver subsided, Solomon collapsed against Ophelia. Their labored breathing comingled, but when their gazes met again, they fluttered weak smiles at one another.

Tell her you love her. Solomon drew a deep breath and opened his mouth...

The bed buckled, and the box spring and mattress— not to mention the newly acquainted lovers—hit the floor.

Ophelia cried out, glanced back at Solomon, and then erupted with laughter.

The tender moment had passed him by, but the night was still young.

Back to the present

Solomon splashed cold water against his face in a sad attempt to wipe the memory of Ophelia's twenty-first birthday out of his head. Of course that was probably his problem; he could never forget. Yet, it pissed him off how easily she could.

He took another splash and had to admit that wasn't exactly true. From time to time, references to their one night together were usually a tag to some joke or toss-away line that friends did to tease one another.

With the exception of her roommate, Kailua, no one else knew about that night, including the third muske-teer—Marcel.

The alarm clock blared from the bedroom, and Solomon casually reached for the towel to dry his face. Calmly, he strolled back into his bedroom, eased onto the edge of the bed, and shut off the alarm.

The morning's soft sunlight streamed through the large windows and kissed his face, but it failed to warm him. What was he going to do now? How could he possibly face a life without Ophelia?

There was nothing left of his heart to break. It had shattered hours ago when she'd last called. A low chuckle escaped him. He'd never pursued a serious relationship with Ophelia for fear of the off chance it could cost them their friendship—and he'd still lost it.

"I just can't win for losing," he mumbled.

You should have told her that night. Solomon nodded to the little voice in his head. No one ever gets anywhere by playing it safe. He knew that. It had certainly applied to his business, and it sure as hell applied now.

He stood and walked over to the window, and gazed out at the landscape of his estate. In no time at all his mind drifted back to that wonderful night.

"How about that champagne now?" Ophelia giggled and sat up in bed. Of course, now they had to reach up for the bottle and cheap wineglasses.

"I wish you'd thought to bring an oxygen tank," Solomon moaned. "I think you're trying to kill me."

"Come on, Mr. Two-time Football Champion. You should know that what doesn't kill you makes you stronger."

She wiggled her rump against him, and his long shaft instantly hardened and throbbed.

Yeah, she was going to be the death of him.

"Shall we make a toast?" she asked, handing him the bottle and corkscrew.

He accepted the items from her. "What would you like to toast to?"

"How about to me for no longer being the last virgin on campus?" She laughed with a roll of her eyes.

Solomon frowned. "What was so bad about being a virgin? What happened to wanting to wait until your wedding night?"

"Did you wait?" she challenged.

Solomon froze at the note of irritability in her tone. "Men aren't the ones that are supposed to wait. That's just setting the stage for disaster if neither party knows what the hell they're doing."

She stared at him as though he had grown another head. "If the men aren't supposed to wait and the women are, then who exactly are the men doing it with?"

He opened his mouth to respond, but words failed him.

"Uh-huh." She crossed her arms. "You were the last person I thought would be sexist."

Solomon could tell a rant was coming on. Such things kept happening since she signed up for women's studies this part quarter. Before she revved up, he could only think to do one thing.

He kissed her.

A second later, he popped the champagne cork. Ophelia and Solomon sprang apart, trying to escape the bubbly's flow. Another round of laughter erupted and they finally managed to get some of the champagne into the two glasses.

"To you no longer being a virgin." Solomon held up his glass.

"And to you for accepting my one-night-only invitation." She clinked their glasses together and then eagerly took a sip.

Solomon didn't.

Her eyes sought his before she lowered her glass. "What's the matter?"

"Seems there was a clause you didn't tell me about."

"What, this being a one-time thing?" she questioned with a small smile.

"Yeah, that."

"Well, I thought that would have been obvious. I mean…can you imagine *us* being a couple?" She laughed.

He gave a halfhearted chuckle. "You know, most women like to kiss, cuddle, and murmur sweet nothings after sex. You, on the other hand, really know how to hit a man where it hurts."

Ophelia blinked and then returned her glass to the nightstand. "No, no. The sex is wonderful."

"Gee. Thanks."

"But come on. Let's be practical. We're young, still in college. You still have wild oats to sow, I might have a few of my own."

"Who the hell teaches those damn classes you're taking?"

She sat her glass on the floor and then turned to caress his face.

He stilled her hand. "I'm starting to feel as though I've been used."

She laughed again. "Don't be silly. I'm just being practical."

"There's that word again."

She sighed and held his steady gaze. "We've been friends a long time, Sol. You know I've always been pretty straight with you. But do you know how many adolescent relationships survive college?"

"No. But I'm sure you do." He sighed, and then downed his drink in one gulp.

"As a matter of fact, I do. Half of one percent. Like those odds?"

Groaning, Solomon turned to climb out of bed.

"Wait. Where are you going?"

"Home. We're done here, aren't we?" He grabbed his boxers.

"You're mad."

"I'm not mad." He stood up.

Ophelia flung the sheets back, crawled over to his side of the bed, and tapped his firm buttocks before he slid on his boxers. "So it's happening already?"

He glanced back at her. Her beautiful nude body left him spellbound and prevented him from moving another inch. "What's happening?"

"Sex is already changing us? Are you going to leave and never speak to me again just because I'm being honest?"

"Of course not."

Her delicately arched eyebrows rose. "This was the only con I could think of before asking you to come here tonight—the fear that sex could cost us our friendship, never mind what would happen if a love affair soured. You mean too much to me. I'd rather have you in my life as a friend than not at all. What about you?"

Solomon stared at her, barely able to breathe because of the painful throb in his chest.

"Stay," she urged.

His throat constricted, and he allowed her to pull him toward her.

"Just for the night," she whispered. "And no one will ever have to know."

He lost himself in her sweet kisses and soft curves. If this was the only night he had, he might as well make the most of it.

And he did just that.

Intermission

Chapter 17

Back at the Crown Room

Toni thanked the bartender for replacing her drink before settling her gaze back on the handsome man beside her. "So far, this sounds like one hell of a triangle."

"Sometimes love gives you more than you bargained for."

"So I've been told," she whispered, taking a sip of her drink.

"You've never been in love?" he asked.

The question threw her off guard. At age forty, Toni had dated many men—from all walks of life. Some men had showed her a good time, others had taught her life lessons, and the rest she'd rather forget.

"I'm going to take that as no." He chuckled.

"Well, it's not that I don't believe in love or anything," she said. "But I've never experienced a lightning bolt or stared into the depths of a man's eyes and felt beyond a shadow of a doubt that I'd met my soul mate." Toni laughed it off, but she was crushed by a wave of disappointment. She had come close once, but close didn't count.

"Then consider yourself lucky," he mumbled.

She didn't feel so lucky. While she was out leaping tall buildings in a single bound, most of her friends had settled down and started families. Meanwhile, she couldn't decide whether owning a dog was too much of a commitment.

"Flight 2193 is now ready for boarding. Flight 2193."

Toni sighed. At this rate, she should've just taken a taxi to Los Angeles. "So what happened next?" she asked, reaching for her glass. "I have to admit I'm intrigued."

"And here I thought I was boring you."

"Not hardly." She nudged him. "Go on. I'm dying to know how this all played out."

He glanced at his watch and gave a half shrug. "All right. Let's see. What happened next?"

Do You Want Him, or Do You Want Me?

Chapter 18

"Oh, Jonas. It's beautiful." Ophelia pressed a hand against her mouth as she stared at the magnificent blue diamond.

"I'm glad you like it." Jonas puffed out his chest while watching his fiancée's eyes gloss with fresh tears. He was glad he chose to present her with the ring over breakfast. The sooner they were able to put last night behind them, the better. "Trust me. The diamond pales in comparison to you."

She cocked her head and looked up at him.

"Poured on a bit thick?" he asked with an uneven smile.

"Just a bit, but it was still nice to hear."

Jonas smiled, extracted the ring from its burgundy box, and then reached for her hand. Pride filled him as the ring slid onto her long finger and sparkled beneath the morning light.

Seeing her reaction did ease some of his guilt. The moment he saw her this morning, he noticed the puffy bags and the tinge of redness in her eyes. She had been crying, most likely over his walking out.

"Seems like the only formality left is for me to talk with your father," he joked.

Ophelia responded with a soft laugh. "Oh, yes. Time to meet the parents. I'm nervous about meeting yours, too."

"Well, I'm sure my parents are going to love you."

She smiled, but then drew a deep breath. "I wish I could say the same."

Jonas frowned. "What do you mean? I've already met your mother. I thought she liked me?"

"Oh, she does." She pressed a reassuring hand against his. "It's my father you're going to have to worry about. Well, you shouldn't worry—he's not going to like you."

"That's encouraging." He frowned.

"Hey, last Christmas was the first time he called Marcel by his name. Before then, he was just referred to as 'young man.'"

"What about Solomon?"

"Young man number two. A lot of times it was just a toss-up as to who he was talking to."

"I...see." Jonas's worried expression intensified.

"He's just a little overprotective. That's all."

"Overprotective? Then how did he allow you to go gallivanting off to Cancun to room with two boys?"

"Oh, yeah." She rolled her eyes skyward. "You probably shouldn't mention that. To this day, he thinks I went to visit a cousin out in California."

Jonas plopped back into his chair and just stared at her. "Uh-huh. Did you lie to your father often?"

"It wasn't a complete lie. Before we came back, I

swung by my cousin Amy's house for a day or two. It's more like I elected not to tell my father everything. He's a strict retired marine who would've skinned the three of us alive, even to this day, if he ever found out the truth."

He knew he was going to hate this, but he had to ask, "Were there any other grand adventures you took with Marcel and Solomon that you didn't tell your father about?"

"Yeah. All of them."

Jonas stiffened. *Just how many were there?*

"But the point is," she said, squeezing his hand, "that there won't be any more secret trips. We've all grown up and have chosen our life partners—"

"A seven-year affair with a married woman hardly qualifies as a life partner," he sniped.

She lowered her gaze and stared at her ring. "Maybe, maybe not. We shouldn't judge," she said quietly.

Jonas grew uncomfortable in the thickening silence. "Anyway, I'm sure I'll be able to win your father over. A lot of people think I'm charming."

She fluttered a brief smile. "You are that. You won me over."

"Have I?" The two simple words held a lot of weight and meaning to them, and Jonas was determined to hold her golden gaze until he had an answer.

"I'm still here, aren't I?" she answered with a question of her own. Then she drew a deep breath and thrust up her chin. "About last night."

He clenched his teeth. He knew they would have to discuss this, but he preferred to just forget the whole thing. "Yes. What about it?"

"You walked out on me."

"Yes, I know—"

"Don't ever do it again," she warned.

Jonas's brows rose in surprise at her hard tone. He wasn't accustomed to being told what to do, or even being challenged, for that matter.

"If there's something wrong," she said, softening her tone, "we talk about it. It's important we agree to this, or we're not going to make it."

Staring into her direct gaze, Jonas suddenly felt as though he was balancing on a thin thread. If he made the wrong move, there was a good chance she would be handing the ring back. However, he needed something to be resolved as well.

"Then let's talk now," he said evenly. "I don't like Solomon. I don't trust him."

"Then you don't trust me."

"And I don't believe you've told me everything that has happened between you two," he added, ignoring her comment. "But at this point, I'm not sure I want to know."

A swift silence ensued.

"Two great things about the past," he continued. "One: we all have them. And two: it *is* the past." He waited until he was certain she caught his meaning. "If Solomon continues to stay around, then I agree with you… We're *not* going to make it."

Ophelia's attention, once again, returned to the ring, sparkling on her finger.

Jonas's heart squeezed at her look of indiscretion. He had hoped for immediate pacification or denial, but it was clear now he would get neither. "O-o-okay." He crossed his arms. "I have to leave for L.A. today," he continued thickly. "Why don't you take a few days to really think this over? Either you're going to be my wife or Solomon's best friend. You can't be both."

* * *

Solomon was the first to arrive at T & B Entertainment. He had a ton of paperwork to catch up on, a couple of acts to review, and a few meetings to conduct. From here on out, he wasn't going to sweat things he couldn't control. If Ophelia wanted to toss their twenty-five-year relationship out of the window, so be it. He had a company to run.

After doling out a greeting to Frank, the half-asleep security guard on duty, Solomon headed to the elevator bay. He loved the office at this time of morning. He tended to get more done when it was quiet.

However, he was somewhat surprised when he entered his office to the sound of a ringing phone. Maybe it would be quick, he rationalized, and then crossed the large office in a few quick strides. "Bassett," he answered.

"I knew your butt would be in the office this early," Selma's disappointed voice filled the line.

"Well, you know how much I hate to disappoint the ladies." He chuckled while sliding off his jacket. "Where are you?"

"Waiting to board my plane," she huffed. "Did you talk to Ophelia yet?"

His hand tightened on the phone as he lowered into his chair. "Yeah. We talked—or more like, she said what she had to say."

"Did you tell her the truth about us?" Concern edged its way into her voice.

"The subject never came up." His throat tightened, forcing him to conclude the conversation. "Look, Selma. I have a lot of work I have to take care of today. Why don't you just give me a call after you make it home?"

"Sol, what happened?"

"I have meetings and auditions lined up," he went on, rubbing his chest. "We can talk about this at another time."

For a moment, the only sound over the line was the busy Hartsfield-Jackson airport. When she finally responded, her voice was soft and maternal. "You promise we'll talk later?"

He didn't want to promise anything. "We'll talk." After disconnecting the call, Solomon eased back in his chair and just stared at the phone. The desire to call Ophelia was strong, however, his head overruled his heart.

The rest of the morning sped by, and just like he'd promised himself, he let the job consume him.

Some time after lunch, news reached him of Zandra Holloway blowing up the coffeemaker. He wasn't quite sure how someone could manage that, but by midafternoon, the woman added a fax and a copier machine to her list of disasters.

"Someone has to talk to her," Chelsea said edgily, jabbing her hands on her waist and tapping her foot. "Someone, meaning *you*."

"Just get someone to show her how to work these things." He forced calmness in his voice and then continued to pore over the profit-and-loss statements.

"I've already tried that," Chelsea sniped.

"Damn it! Do I have to do everything around here?" he exploded.

His secretary blinked and took a retreating step.

"Seriously, Chelsea, do you think as vice president of a Fortune 500 company, I should be the one teaching employees how to use a fax machine?"

"N-no, sir." She stared at him open-mouthed. "I'll take care of it."

"Thank you." He watched her with teeth still clenched while she made her escape; but his annoyance refused to wane for a few hours.

The good thing was everyone left him alone after that. When he walked down the halls, the employees went out of their way to avoid crossing his path. Today, that suited him just fine.

"Mr. Bassett?" Chelsea's stiff but professional voice floated over the intercom at exactly five o'clock.

"Yes?"

"I have a call for you on line one."

"Who is it?"

"Ms. Missler."

Solomon looked up from his piles of reports to stare at the phone.

"Should I put the call through?" Chelsea asked.

He winced at the sudden pain in his chest, but his gaze remained glued to the phone. The battle between his heart and head turned into a full-scale war. The victor won only by a narrow margin.

"Mr. Bassett?"

Finally, he snatched up the phone while ice poured through his veins. "Tell Ms. Missler I've left for the day."

Chapter 19

As always, Solomon was given the full VIP treatment when he entered Club Secrets. For one night only, the dance club was putting on a talent search à la *American Idol*. The prize was a one-single deal with T & B Entertainment. Needless to say, he really wasn't in the mood for this.

And sure enough, his time and patience were wasted. Most of the acts couldn't even win a karaoke contest, let alone a serious talent search. Solomon's good friend and the club's owners, Tee Bo, at least mumbled his apologies and claimed it was also his first time hearing the performers.

However, since the event drew a large crowd, Tee Bo vowed to hold another contest in the near future.

"You're going to have to get another label, man," Solomon said. "Get Jermaine Dupri or somebody. I can't do this again. Maybe he's looking for someone." His candor obviously took Tee Bo by surprise. Between Marcel and Solomon, Solomon was usually the one who let people down easy.

Not tonight.

Minutes after the contest, the stage was cleared, the loud music returned, and dancers crowded the floor. While Solomon's mood continued to spiral downward, he felt his cell phone vibrate against his leg. He scooped it out of his pocket and glanced at the caller ID screen.

Ophelia Missler.

He stared at the name while the phone continued to vibrate. When it stopped, he simply returned the phone to his pocket and then ordered a drink from a passing waitress.

Several drinks later, he was finally starting to loosen up, and was feeling pretty good. Damn good, in fact.

A few hot ladies from the dance floor gave him come-hither looks, while they gyrated to a new Usher hit. He was only too happy to accompany them.

Talk about feeling like a kid in a candy store. In no time at all, Solomon was surrounded and proving that at thirty-five, he still had a few smooth dance moves left.

Whenever he felt the buzz of his cell phone, the harder he danced and the more he drank. Tonight he was going to take a page out of his uncle's playbook and have a little fun—and these ladies were going to be the ones to show him how.

Ophelia needed to apologize—to the point of desperation. But with every unanswered phone call, her anxiety intensified, causing a slight pain in her chest.

He was ignoring her calls, she was certain of it.

She brought this on herself, she realized, which made the pill that much harder to swallow. Her gaze fell to her hand and the heavy diamond ring pressed against her finger.

Extremely heavy.

"This is wrong," she whispered, and then immediately tried to snatch the thing off her finger. It wouldn't budge.

"Damn it." She jumped to her feet and stormed away from the tons of swatches, menus, and magazines that she and Kailua had spent hours poring over. There were too many choices and too many decisions involved in planning a wedding. So many, in fact, it was a wonder that anyone ever made it to the altar.

Ophelia rushed into one of the downstairs bathrooms and turned on the faucet full blast. Plunging her hands beneath the stream of water, she tried again to pull the ring off.

It still wouldn't budge.

"Oh, come on." She gritted her teeth and pulled with all her might. It was more likely she would snap her finger off before the ring ever came loose.

"Oh, forget it," she panted, giving up. The damn thing felt as if it were welded on. As she turned off the faucet, she locked gazes with her reflection in the mirror.

"What the hell am I doing?" she asked. She paused, as if waiting for an answer, and then slumped forward.

Jonas was right. She wasn't being honest—with him, with herself, or with Solomon. But what was the truth? she wondered.

Was she in love with Solomon?

Or was Jonas saying it so much that she was starting to believe it?

How could she have told Solomon that she never

wanted to see him again? And how could she have even considered Jonas's ultimatum?

"I have to fix this," she whispered, turning to leave the bathroom. Minutes later, she was in her car, speeding toward Solomon's place. Her mind raced with all the things she needed to say.

Of course Solomon would forgive her. This wasn't the first time in their twenty-five-year history that she had done something stupid.

What if he doesn't? The dubious voice in her head was so loud that she glanced up at her reflection in the rearview mirror. The pain in her chest returned, and she reached a hand over to her purse to check and see if she had some Tums or Rolaids. No such luck.

Why wouldn't Solomon forgive her? He forgave her when she toilet papered his car, and when she accidentally gave him a black eye during a sparring match for charity—of course, it was his fault for trying to take it easy on her. The point was, Solomon always forgave her. He looked after her, cared for her, and had always been there.

Well, I love you, too, and look where the hell that has gotten me.

Ophelia's foot eased up on the accelerator as Solomon's voice rang in her head. Could it be that she, practical Ophelia, had overlooked the obvious? The old saying that you don't know what you've got until it's gone came to mind, and she was suddenly nauseous with fear.

At every point of their lives, she was able to rationalize or unearth some new statistic as to why a relationship with Solomon would never work. In college it was the "sow the wild oats" speech and the "low percentage of high school sweethearts surviving campus life." In their mid-twenties, Marcel and Solomon had gone into the entertainment field, and the odds of a relationship's survival dipped so low on the chart that it was laughable.

Why subject herself to worrying about ambitious female artists and groupies when she knew she couldn't handle it? She had a hard enough time letting him go the morning after her twenty-first birthday. She should have received an Academy Award for that performance.

It hurt like hell.

But did any of this mean that she was *in* love with Solomon? "What's not to love?" she whispered, and then felt the threat of tears rise from the backs of her eyes.

Her cell phone rang, and she nearly jumped clear out of her skin. She reached for her purse again and then swiped out her cell phone. "Solomon, where the hell are you?"

A long pause, and then, "This is Jonas," he said thickly.

Her heart dropped. That was what she got for not reading the caller-ID screen. "Oh, hi…sweetheart."

There was another long pause before Jonas's stiff tone returned to the line. "I was just calling to let you know I'd just checked in at the Beverly Wilshire, but I see you were expecting another call."

She didn't answer. What could she say?

"Anyway, I'm in room 623 if you need anything."

"Jonas—"

"I'm going to hit the shower. I'll talk to you later," he said, and then disconnected the call.

Ophelia held the silent phone a few seconds longer, and then finally, after mumbling a few curses she flipped it closed. She was almost afraid to ask if things could get any worse.

Solomon's estate came into view, and by the time she reached the gate, she still didn't have a clue as to what to say. And what was she going to tell Jonas after this? Undoubtedly, she would suffer through more accusations of her being in love with Solomon, which was ridiculous.

Wasn't it?

She entered the security code and waited patiently for the gate to open.

"Am I in love with Solomon?"

Driving onto the property, she took her time going down the long, curvy pathway to the main house. She glanced at the clock in her car and frowned. It was nearly three in the morning. It was definitely too late to be visiting.

And yet she didn't turn around. "Am I in love with him?" She sat still and listened to her own breathing while laboring over the question. However, it didn't take long before an answer tumbled faintly from her lips.

"Yes."

Sighing in relief, she glanced up at Solomon's large home. A few of the lights were still on in the house. Maybe there was a good chance Solomon was still up.

She opened her car door and stepped out into the cool morning air. Her knees trembled and her stomach twisted into knots as she approached the door. She still had no clue as to what she was going to say or what she was going to do if he refused to speak with her.

"Of course he'll speak to you." She forced up her confidence, rang the doorbell, and waited.

The wind picked up velocity, rustled her hair, and sent a cold shiver down her spine. After a while, she tried the bell again.

No answer.

Disappointed, she turned and walked down the steps. She supposed he could be out of town, but she really wished she could talk to him tonight.

Music suddenly caught her ear, and she turned to glance back at the door. *He's home?*

Walking back, she dug through her purse, retrieved her spare key, and entered the house.

"Hello?" she called out from the foyer.

Nothing but music drifted back to her. Curious, Ophelia followed the sound, periodically saying, "Hello."

Giggles reached her ears at the same moment she stopped inside the archway to the living room. Three barely dressed women stopped dancing to gape at her.

Solomon's deep baritone drifted from somewhere, while his footsteps drew louder. "Looks like we're in luck, ladies. You'll never guess what I found down in the wine cellar." He stopped at the archway on the other side of the living room and glanced up. His smile froze in place. "Ophelia?"

Her face heated with embarrassment. "I—I guess this is a bad time." Her faint smile quivered before she turned and walked away.

"Wait!"

She quickened her stride at the sound of Solomon racing behind her. It didn't help. He still caught up with her before she slipped out.

"Ophelia, wait."

His hand clenched her arm and spun her around.

She lost her balance and fell against him. His chest was rock hard, just like it was back in college. She pushed him away, ignoring how her body seemed to short-circuit in his close presence.

"What are you doing here?" he asked.

Staring up into his dark eyes, she suddenly lost the ability to speak.

Solomon's frown deepened. "Ophelia?"

Regaining some of her equilibrium, she forced on another smile. "I wanted to talk to you."

He loosened his hold. After a few strained seconds of silence, he said, "So talk."

Uncomfortable about being put on the spot and worried about the hard glint in his eyes, she concluded, "Maybe I should come back at another time."

"I'm not busy at the moment."

Her brows rose. "You have company."

"They can wait."

"Where's Selma?"

"She went home."

Ophelia pulled her arm away and squared her shoulders. *Just say it.* "I came over to tell you that—"

"Solomon," a feminine voice sing-songed across the foyer.

Ophelia and Solomon turned. One of his ladies in waiting stood proudly before them in only a pair of low-cut panties.

"The girls are getting a little anxious." The woman twirled her long hair around her fingers as her gaze shifted to Ophelia. "Is she joining us?"

"I don't think so," Ophelia sneered, and then glared at Solomon. "I was just leaving."

He didn't stop her.

Bolting through the door, she made sure that it slammed behind her. "He's just like his damn uncle," she seethed, marching to her car.

The wind howled, and a few droplets of water splattered against her face. However, it wasn't until she slid in behind the wheel that she realized it wasn't raining.

"I'm such an idiot." She started the car and quickly wiped her eyes. Ms. Practical Ophelia almost made the biggest mistake of her life. She was going to tell Solomon she was in love with him.

She emitted a sad chuckle and pressed her foot on the accelerator. "What the hell was I thinking?"

You are a part of our lives; please be a part of our special day.
You are cordially invited to be with us on the occasion of a celebration of a miracle...love, when we, Ophelia Missler and Jonas Hinton, join together in marriage on Saturday, the twelfth of November.

Chapter 20

On a mid-October morning, Diana Taylor's eyes skimmed over the wedding invitation several times before she turned from the foyer table and strolled through the wide space of her Georgia suburban mansion in search of her husband.

She found Marcel in the backyard, running around with the other girl in his life: Brandy. At first sight of them frolicking around, her quick strides slowed, and then she stopped to lean against the back door.

Diana loved listening to her husband's laughter and Brandy's rambunctious barking. Of course, this wasn't always so. Up until a year ago, she was terrified of dogs, Brandy especially. In fact, the first time she had any dealings with the lovable dog, Diana had found herself cowering at the bottom of a closet.

She laughed at the memory and, in turn, drew Marcel's and Brandy's attention. Her body tingled the moment his gaze centered on her and then warmed when he smiled. Who knew that life could be so perfect?

A few seconds later, Marcel rushed up to her and swept her into his strong embrace. It was like being enfolded in a nice, strong, comfortable blanket—one she wished she never had to take off.

"It looks like Ophelia is going through with this." Diana waved the invitation in front of him.

He groaned and rolled his eyes. "I like Jonas but..."

Diana sighed and laid her head against her husband's chest. "Are they still not talking to each other?"

"Three months and counting." Disappointment laced Marcel's words. "Maybe it's time for an intervention."

She pulled back and glanced up at him. "Do you really think that's wise?"

He shrugged. "They're my best friends."

"Yeah, but Jonas doesn't want Solomon in the picture."

"Which is another reason why I don't like the guy." Marcel's face darkened. "What if he'd said that he didn't want her associating with me? Would she have given me the heave-ho, too?"

"So are you mad at him or Ophelia?"

"Both," he snapped.

Diana rubbed his back to encourage him to calm down. "I haven't known them as long as you have, but maybe there's something more going on than we know. Ophelia seems to be like a very practical woman."

"Too practical for her own good, if you ask me."

"Maybe we need to face up to the fact that maybe she's really in love with Jonas...and that Solomon has missed his chance."

Marcel was silent for a long time before he said, "Yeah. Maybe you're right."

* * *

Solomon had a difficult time paying attention in his meeting. He wasn't even sure what the damn thing was about. His thoughts were preoccupied with the wedding invitation that was accidentally mailed to him.

Or maybe it was a peace offering.

Either way, he had no intention of attending.

It had been three months since he'd last seen or spoken to Ophelia. Three months since he had constructed the perfect wall around his heart. However, the invitation delivered a serious blow and even managed to cause serious damage.

For the millionth time, he reviewed the morning she appeared at his place. She had started to tell him something but was interrupted. Wondering what that something was had become an obsession.

The way she stormed out, however, left a sour taste in his mouth. A part of him wanted to chase after her; the other part was tired of it. She had made her choice and, come hell or high water, he was going to honor it.

When the meeting adjourned, he managed to flash the drifting employees a plastic smile; but he remained rooted in his chair long after everyone had left. Leaning back, he swiveled toward the large, wall-length windows to stare out at the city landscape.

He needed a change.

After the thought drifted across his mind, he nearly laughed out loud. Wasn't that the same thing Marcel spouted shortly before he fell in love and got married?

Maybe that's what he needed—to find a nice girl and settle down. It seemed to have worked wonders for Marcel. The man was positively glowing and cracking jokes at every possible turn. Quite frankly, it was starting to get on Solomon's nerves.

Then there was the possibility of transferring to T & B's New York office. There was no longer any point of both him and Marcel working out of Atlanta.

The more Solomon thought about it, the more he liked the idea. A change—that was exactly what he needed.

The conference room's door bolted open, and Marcel poked his head inside. "There you are. I've been looking all over the place for you. Your uncle's here, stirrin' up trouble. Can you handle it before we get slammed with sexual harassment suits?"

Solomon groaned, propped his elbows up on the table, and buried his face in his hand. "Lord, please, not today."

"Well, I can always call security," Marcel joked.

Moaning, Solomon pushed himself out of his chair. "As tempting as that offer may be, I have a feeling that I'd never live it down."

"That makes two of us." Marcel stared at Solomon as he approached the door. "You all right, man?"

"Never better," Solomon lied, but he was forced to stop in his tracks when his friend blocked the exit.

Marcel slid his hands into his pockets and rocked back on his heels. "Not to get all mushy on you or anything—"

"Then don't," Solomon huffed, meeting his friend's level gaze.

If his buddy was put off or surprised by his surliness, Marcel didn't show it, nor did he step away from the door. "You know, Diana and I have invited Jonas and Ophelia over for dinner. Why don't you stop by? We'd love to have you."

Solomon laughed. "Nice try, but I'll pass."

"How long are you two going to keep this up? It's ridiculous."

Drawing a deep breath, Solomon squared his shoulders. "I really do appreciate the concern, but it's not necessary. I'm a big boy. I'll be fine."

Gazes still locked, Marcel nodded, and then finally stepped aside.

Solomon crossed the threshold and stopped again. "I'm thinking about moving to our offices in New York." He shrugged with a casualness he didn't feel. "I'll keep you posted."

This time, Marcel blinked in surprise. "We'll certainly miss you around here. But if you gotta go, you gotta go. I understand."

Solomon met his gaze again, nodded, and then strolled off. Minutes later, a woman's hysterical scream pierced his eardrum, and he raced to find out what was happening. What he found was the makings of World War III.

"You bastard! I'm going to kill you," Nora Gibson screeched, struggling to reach his Uncle Willy.

Luckily, there were six other women fighting equally hard to keep her back.

"I was still going to call," Willy said, shrugging and smirking. "I've just been tied up…literally."

Just great. Solomon moaned and approached the scene with a rising furor. "Ms. Gibson, get a hold of yourself," he thundered.

Everyone froze.

Nora's angry glare landed on him, but quickly cooled when Solomon gave one of his own.

"Now what the hell is going on here?" he asked the circle of employees.

Uncle Willy stepped forward with a cocksure grin

and his chest puffed up. "Oh, it nothing, li'l nephew." He slid his arm around Nora's waist and squeezed her close. "It's just a little lover's spat." He winked and unfortunately didn't see that right hook Nora sent his way.

The women gasped, Willy went down for the count, and Nora stormed off, mumbling, "Selfish bastard!"

All in all, it was the highlight of Solomon's day.

The security guards came and helped prop Willy on the couch in Solomon's office. Chelsea was kind enough to make an ice pack for his eye, and Solomon made him a drink.

"Ooh, that's going to leave a mark," Chelsea said while inspecting Nora's work.

"Hey, you don't need an excuse to get close to me." Willy smiled and slapped his knees. "Just pop a squat, sweetheart. I'll take you on a ride you'll never forget."

Chelsea dropped the ice pack back on his eye and smiled when he yelped in pain. "Keep it up, and I'll blacken the other one for you."

Willy's boisterous laugh followed her out of the room.

Solomon sighed and shook his head as he sat behind his desk. "I'm sorry to have to do this to you, Uncle Willy, but I'm going to have to ask you to not come by the office anymore."

"Aw, come on. That was nothing." Willy chuckled, reaching into his pocket and removing a cigar.

"This is a place of business not the W.W.E." Solomon eased back in his chair and folded his arms. "You're loud and obnoxious—"

"I've never claimed to be an angel—"

"You offend the female staff—"

"Oh, they love me. Don't let them tell you otherwise." He stuck the cigar in his mouth.

"Don't smoke in here."

"Hey, a buddy of mine is throwing a party next weekend. You wanna come?" He lit the cigar.

Solomon's eyes narrowed as he pushed out of his chair and walked around the desk. "I said, no smoking." He removed the cigar from his uncle's mouth and dropped it into Willy's drink.

"Hey!"

"Hey, yourself, old man," he snapped back, and then drew a deep breath. "How do you do it?"

Willy set his ruined drink down on a nearby table. "How do I do what?"

"Just breeze through life, going from one party after another—drifting from one woman to another." Solomon tossed up his hands. "I mean, what is that? Is this fun for you? Tell me, because I must be missing something. Boxing, stabbings, shootings—aren't you getting a little too old for this crap?"

Willy looked at him like he'd never seen him before.

As the silence thickened, Solomon, too, began to see cracks in his uncle's happy mask. Sadness dulled his eyes, and signs of weariness surfaced from nowhere.

"Not everyone has what you have," his uncle said dully. "Or should I say, what you could've had?"

Solomon thrust up his chin.

"I, unfortunately, never ran across a soul mate. And believe it or not, I've looked for her from time to time." He chuckled and then drew a long breath. "Now, my brother—your father, on the other hand, was just like you. When he was eight, he fell in love with a cute little girl next door to us. The entire family used to laugh at how he would follow this girl around like a long lost puppy. He'd carry her books to school, create homemade valentine cards, and taken her to every school dance.

This continued through junior high and high school. They were inseparable."

Enthralled, Solomon leaned back against his desk and asked, "What happened?"

Willy shrugged. "When he turned eighteen, he enlisted in the army and married her."

"Mom?"

"Yep. Your mother. He was the luckiest sonofabitch I ever knew. That is, until you came along." Willy met Solomon's gaze. "Course, we know you story is going to turn out a little bit different, don't we?"

Solomon's chest tightened. "You don't know what you're talking about."

Willy stood up, handed over his ice pack, and adjusted his jacket to leave. "Yeah. You just keep telling yourself that."

Chapter 21

"I'm having a lot of chest pain," Ophelia complained to her doctor while perched on an examining table.

Dr. Thomas, a handsome African-American internist, scrunched up his face with instant concern and asked, "Show me where you're having the pain."

Ophelia obligingly pointed to the area just above her heart. "It doesn't hurt all the time, which is why it might be indigestion."

"Are you feeling any pain right now?" the doctor asked, flipping open her chart.

"No, not right now. It sort of comes and goes." Suddenly, she felt silly for even bringing it up; but as long as she was there for a physical, she might as well mention it.

"Are you under any type of stress—maybe work related—?"

"I'm getting married in less than a month," Ophelia offered.

"That will do it." Dr. Thomas's expression relaxed to an easy smile. "What you're experiencing is likely a combination of stress and anxiety. It's actually pretty normal, but do try to do some activities that are going to relax you. Stress can cause major damage to your body."

Ophelia nodded. *Stress, yeah.* Why hadn't she thought of that? Maybe she would relieve some stress if she could decide on a dress. Four weeks until the wedding, and she had two wedding dresses. Actually, she seemed to have trouble deciding on everything. Jonas had picked out the wedding colors (blue and white), the wedding location (Château Élan), the menus, and the cake.

And sad to say, her mother and Kailua had picked out Jonas's wedding band—though she had narrowed it down to four. The whole thing was pathetic. All her life, she had been praised for her organizational and managing skills, but when it came to her own wedding, she was a blank and more than willing to let others take over.

All she had to do was show up.

Of course, sex was a great stress reliever, too. Maybe she was tense because she wasn't getting any until her wedding night.

"Now, there's a thought," she mumbled under her breath. Driving through downtown, Ophelia's eyes were drawn to T & B Entertainment's office building. Fleetingly, she wondered what the guys were doing—more specifically, what Solomon was doing.

Three months, she thought sadly. She didn't intend for so much time to pass, despite the ultimatum from her fiancé. It's just that each day it grew harder to muster an apology. Then she began to hope that Solomon would call her.

He never did.

Solomon wasn't going to be a part of the wedding—hell, he'd failed to RSVP after receiving his invite. Then again, what did she expect?

Ophelia turned her gaze from the glass office building and then slammed on her brakes. Despite the loud screeching, she still managed to tap the bumper of the car ahead of her. She cringed when she noticed it was a black S-series Mercedes, but her gaze also skimmed across the personalized license plate: SGRDADY.

"Uncle Willy."

The Mercedes's door opened, and the familiar profile of the often rude and crass but lovable Uncle Willy squeezed out of his car. He strolled to the back while the rest of the traffic maneuvered around them.

As he inspected his bumper, Ophelia also climbed out of her car, wearing a wide smile.

"Well, well, well," Willy boasted and stretched his arms wide. "It's the little filly that got away."

Unsure of what he meant, she still allowed him to sweep her into a bear hug.

"You know, I still haven't received my invitation to this glamorous wedding I keep hearing about. Don't make me lay you across my lap and give a good spanking. You know how much I like parties."

Laughing, Ophelia pushed out of his embrace. "Then consider yourself personally invited."

Willy's smile broadened. "Well, can I put you over my lap anyway?"

She tossed her head back with a hearty laugh. "You're still a riot," she complimented. "Don't ever change."

"You have my word on it." He winked. "So how do you want to work off the damage to my car?"

"Is it bad?" She rushed around him to take a peek for herself. Yet, when she leaned forward for an inspection, she couldn't find so much as a scratch. "I don't see any damage." She stood and glanced over at him.

"Damn. I could've used a personal sex slave," he said, and snapped his fingers.

"I thought you had plenty of those."

"Hey, you can't blame a guy for trying, right?"

"You can try, but it's never gonna happen, old man." Chuckling, Ophelia rolled her eyes and headed back to her car.

"Are you on your way to see my nephew?"

Her knees weakened and she hurried to slide behind the wheel. "I'm afraid not."

"Mind if I ask why?"

She blinked and stammered for a moment. "I—I'm running some errands today. I'm sure I'll catch up with him another time." Ophelia closed her door.

Willy leaned against it, until she rolled down the window. "You know, I'm a firm believer that you should never put off till tomorrow who you can screw today."

Ophelia laughed and shook her head.

"C'mon. You're here, he's right over there." He held her gaze. "What's a little harmless visit?"

For months now, Jonas had subjected himself to private dance lessons. So far he had learned the waltz, mambo, rumba, and the tango. He wasn't going to win any dance contest, but he was definitely going to be able to impress his wife on their wedding day.

Wife. His chest ballooned with hope for the future. He didn't want to waste any time waiting to have children. He desperately wanted a little girl with Ophelia's beautiful eyes, and a boy who would one day take over his financial empire.

They would have homes around the world, and he would see to it that they had the best of everything. The daydream brought a smile to his face, and a sudden rush of anxiousness for the first day of the rest of their lives together.

However, there was one man who threatened everything: Solomon. Sure, he hadn't heard Ophelia so much as utter his name lately; but the man still had a tangible presence between them.

But for now, he'd gotten his wish. Solomon was out of the picture. Yet something in the back of his mind wondered for how long.

"So, are we ready, Mr. Hinton?" his dance instructor, Cici Castillo, asked, entering the studio.

Jonas stood, took a deep breath, and clapped his hands. "Sure. Let's get started!"

Ophelia parked outside of Solomon's office building and waited for her courage to build. What possible explanation could she offer for not speaking to him? She had decided to sever ties before Jonas's ultimatum. She had made the selfish decision to throw away their twenty-five-year-old relationship.

And she missed him.

"Just go in there, ask for your slice of crow pie, and put everything behind you," she instructed herself. However, she made no move toward the door.

Sighing, she lowered her head against the steering wheel and waded through a flood of emotions. This was one of the hardest things she'd ever had to do. Minutes passed before she finally lifted her head, wiped her eyes dry, and stepped out of the car.

She strolled through the doors, flashing a bright smile to the staff as she made her way toward Solomon's office. But Marcel crossed her path first.

"What are you doing here?" he asked, stealing a hug and a quick kiss.

"I, uh, swung by to see Sol. Is he in?"

Marcel's handsome face lit up. "Ah, finally. I'm glad to see one of you came to your senses."

A rush of embarrassment heated her face, and she didn't quite know what to say.

"Well, he should be in his office. If you want, I can walk down there with you."

"No, no. That's not necessary." She shrugged when Marcel frowned. "This is sort of a…private matter. I'd rather not beg for forgiveness in front of an audience."

Marcel didn't appear to be offended. Instead, he gave her an encouraging wink. "I'm sure everything is going to be fine."

I hope so. She said her goodbyes to Marcel, and promised to see him and Diana later that evening for dinner. However, when she continued her journey toward Solomon's office, she felt like a prisoner taking that final walk toward her execution.

She spotted Chelsea behind her desk and flashed her a quick smile. Since the secretary was on the phone, Ophelia whispered, "Is he in?" while stealthily moving toward Solomon's closed door.

Chelsea quickly hung up the phone and jumped to her feet. "Ms. Missler, I'm sorry, but Mr. Bassett isn't in his office."

Ophelia blinked, taken aback by the woman's forceful tone. "Well, do you mind if I go in and wait for him?"

"He's gone for the day. He left a few minutes ago. I'll make sure to tell him that you stopped by," Chelsea said, with no trace of friendliness in her expression.

A strange tension lapsed between the two women before Ophelia forced herself to nod. "Thanks. I appreciate it."

"No problem." A slow smile finally stretched across the secretary's face.

Hackles high, Ophelia turned and strolled away. She kept her chin up and her plastic smile in place, but humiliation settled and soured in her stomach.

Once she pushed through the building's glass door, she dropped her farcical mask and rushed to her car. She didn't believe Chelsea. Solomon was there, and her guess was that he'd given strict instructions to get rid of her if she ever showed up. Of course, she had no proof of that. It was just an instinct she couldn't shake.

Sliding in behind the steering wheel, she quickly started the car. But before she pulled out of her parking spot, she caught a glimpse of one of Solomon's cars, a silver Porsche, parked in his reserved parking space.

The hole in Ophelia's heart widened, and she feared the damage would never be repaired.

Solomon stood before his office window, staring down at Ophelia's pecan-colored Jaguar. He'd done the right thing, he told himself. Sure, he could've seen her, buried the hatchet, gone back to being best friends. All of that would mean he'd have to stand on the sidelines and watch her marry Jonas, bear his children, and watch them live happily ever after.

Solomon couldn't do that—he wouldn't do that.

The only way to end the emotional roller coaster was

to sever ties. In his heart, he knew he would always love Ophelia. But it was way past time to let go.

After he watched the Jag pull out of the parking lot and merge into traffic, he turned from the window and left the office. He found Marcel at Zandra's cubicle. Both were searching madly for something on her desk.

"You have a minute?" Solomon asked.

"Sure." Marcel sighed, seeming relieved for the interruption.

Zandra nervously braided her hands together. "I'll keep looking for those budget reports, Mr. Taylor. I know they're around here—somewhere."

Marcel drew a weary breath and gestured for Solomon toward his office. Once the men entered and closed the door, Marcel nearly collapsed against it.

"I like Zandra, but she has to go," he grumbled.

"Then fire her."

"I'd love to, but she's a good friend of Diana's grandmother. Every time I even hint that things aren't working out, I'm bombarded with pleas to give the woman another chance. But I don't know how much more I can take."

Solomon shared a sympathetic smile.

"So, what's up, man?" Marcel asked, heading toward his in-office bar. "Can I get you a drink?"

"Nah. I'll pass." Solomon waved off the offer.

"I saw Ophelia a while ago," Marcel said, dropping ice into his glass. "Did you two finally kiss and make up?"

Solomon winced against the pinch in his chest. "Look, I just came by to tell you I made my decision. I'm moving to our New York offices."

Marcel frowned and lowered the rum bottle. After a brief silence, he asked, "When?"

"I'm leaning toward next month."

"That soon?"

Solomon shrugged. "What can I say? I need a change of scenery."

His buddy's gaze narrowed with suspicion. "You didn't talk to her, did you?"

"What would be the point?" he asked simply. "I knew this day would come, and I thought I'd be able to handle it. Turns out—I can't. Now, the only way I'm going to get over her is just simply not to be around." Solomon turned and headed toward the door.

"Don't go, Sol. Come to dinner tonight."

"Give my best to Diana." He faced Marcel and winked. "At least one of us got it right." He turned back toward the door.

"You're making a mistake," Marcel said.

Solomon stopped with his hand on the doorknob. "No. My mistake was not loving her when I had the chance. I didn't take the risk, and I lost her anyway." He chuckled, but it held a note of misery. "That's what you call irony."

Chapter 22

After an evening of dance lessons, Jonas came home to a quiet and distant fiancée. No amount of coaxing would loosen her lips about what was wrong. Yet, he had his suspicions, ones that deepened with each tick of the clock.

Anger and distrust crept up the base of his spine, and before he knew it, they moved around each other in a strange, muted dance on eggshells. By the time they were on the road toward the Taylors, he simply couldn't take it anymore.

"Did you see Solomon today?" he asked, glancing over at her in the passenger seat.

Ophelia rolled her eyes. "Don't start that again."

His grip tightened on the steering wheel while his irritation escalated. Suddenly it was as if Solomon was in the car, sitting between them. Jonas's dreams of the future inched out of his reach.

"No," she whispered and turned her gaze to view the scenery outside her window. "I didn't see him."

Briefly, Jonas closed his eyes and exhaled in relief.

"But it wasn't from lack of trying," she added, her attention still focused elsewhere.

"What is that supposed to mean?" He glanced at her again.

Ophelia drew a deep breath and then turned to meet his steady gaze. "It means I miss my best friend. It means I went to see Solomon, but he refused to talk to me. I hurt him…and it's killing me." Her voice quivered as her eyes glossed with instant tears. "I'm guessing that you're pretty happy about the whole thing."

The misery he read in the depths of her eyes crushed any feelings of victory. It was the lowest he'd ever felt. Causing her this type of pain was never his intention. His gaze lowered, and he noticed how she absently fumbled with her engagement ring.

"You're right. I shouldn't have given you that ultimatum."

Ophelia shook her head. Her tears trickled down her face. "No…you shouldn't have," she said softly. "But I'd made that decision before then."

Jonas frowned. "What do you mean?"

The quivering lips intensified. "That night you stormed out…"

Once again, he closed his eyes, still feeling like the scum of the earth. Yet, he was stuck between a rock and a hard place. He didn't like or trust Solomon, but if he didn't fix this situation, he was going to be blamed for this for the rest of their lives…if he managed to get her down the aisle.

"I'll talk to him," Jonas offered, his gaze still watching her play with her ring.

"I can't expect you to fix my mess," she said. "I did this. I have to handle it—if he'll let me."

"Still, I—"

"We'd better hurry." Ophelia sniffed and held up her head. "We don't want to be late."

The discussion was officially closed. However, Jonas had already made up his mind. He didn't like it, but it appeared that Solomon was vital to the success of his pending marriage.

Damn it.

"What do you mean, Solomon is moving to New York?" Diana asked as she slid on her last earring. "Are you joking?"

"I wish I was." Marcel leaned back against the bedroom wall, and then smiled when his wife stood from her vanity chair. He marveled at her wholesome beauty while she glided toward him in a royal blue dress that complemented her cute, curvy figure.

"So what are we going to do?" she asked, leaning up on her toes.

Marcel was only too happy to heed to her unspoken request for a kiss. Loving the feel of her soft lips, he pulled her pliant body against him and was having thoughts of stripping her out of her clothes.

Diana moaned and slid her arms around his neck. However, she was the only one with a thread of willpower to break their kiss and thus send them both crashing back to earth. "You didn't answer my question," she whispered softly against his lips.

Frowning, he took a moment to recall what they were talking about. "Oh, yeah. Solomon." He maintained his hold on her and shrugged. "I'm not sure there's much we can do. Jonas and Ophelia are going to be living permanently in Atlanta, and Solomon doesn't want to be around. Pure and simple."

"But he loves her. He can't just give up like that."

"Honey, I know. I tried to talk to him this afternoon after Ophelia came by the office."

"So they're talking again?" Diana's face lit up. "That's great."

"It would've been if he'd spoken to her." Marcel shook his head. "This is not going to be an easy fix. Solomon seems determined to walk away." He sighed. "I never thought I'd see this day, but I think it's really over between Solomon and Ophelia."

Diana's grandmother, Louisa Mae, answered the door when Ophelia and Jonas arrived at the Taylor estate. Opening it, she smiled warmly and gestured for Jonas and Ophelia to enter.

"You must be Diana's mother," Jonas teased, pressing a kiss against the older woman's hand.

"Oh, my." Louisa fluttered her free hand against her heart. "Aren't you a handsome charmer?" She cut her gaze to Ophelia. "Better keep an eye on this one. I'm in the market."

The couple laughed as Louisa closed the door behind them.

"My, my, my," Louisa cooed, turning her attention back to them. "You two make such a beautiful couple. Of course, back in the day, either one of my husbands and I would've given you a run for your money. That's because I look good on anyone's arm." She winked.

Ophelia laughed and instantly fell in love with the older woman.

"Wow." Louisa grabbed Ophelia's hands and ogled the large blue diamond on her hand. "Now, that's a ring."

"Well, if it isn't the future Mr. and Mrs. Hinton," Marcel commented as he and his wife strolled into the foyer.

"And if it isn't the former Casanova Brown," Ophelia teased.

"*Former* being the key word," Diana joked, squeezing her husband's waist.

Ophelia greeted Diana with a quick peck on the cheek, and then accepted Marcel's open-arm invitation for a hug. Standing in the folds of his familiar embrace, Ophelia longed to stay, lean on him as she'd done in the past, and seek his advice on how to mend the growing divide between her and Solomon.

Hearing Jonas's small cough, Ophelia eased out of her friend's arms and flashed everyone a stiff smile. The awkward moment passed quickly, and the group of five spilled into the grand living room. Drinks were poured all around, and small talk morphed into genuine conversation.

"So which one of you are experiencing wedding jitters?" Diana asked, after receiving yet another kiss from her doting husband. "I know I was a nervous wreck at ours."

"Don't tell me you were having second thoughts?" Marcel said with an instant frown.

Diana laughed. "Not about marrying you, but whether some scorned woman was going to stand up in the middle of the ceremony during that 'speak now or forever hold your peace' line."

Ophelia laughed, and then tried to look contrite when Marcel turned a hurtful expression toward her. "C'mon, Marcel. We didn't call you Casanova Brown for nothing."

"Well," he said, once again gathering his wife close,

"I'm a changed man now. I've fallen for the perfect woman."

Diana giggled and submitted to another smothering kiss.

Sparks of jealousy flared within Ophelia as she watched the loving couple. At the feel of Jonas's arm drifting around her waist, she fought the sudden urge to pull away. And at the feel of his soft lips against hers, she wished she had.

When it ended, she had her ready-made smile in place. But glancing away, she caught Louisa's curious gaze.

"So," Louisa said, smiling broadly, "you two known each other long?"

"Uh, no, ma'am. We—"

"Oh, honey, please. All my friends call me Lou." She winked.

"All right, Lou," Ophelia amended, and reached for her fiancé's hand. "Jonas and I have known each other for nearly eight months."

"Ooh, must have been one of those love-at-first-sight sort of things," Lou said with twinkling eyes.

"I know it was for me," Jonas said, landing another kiss against Ophelia's cheek.

Ophelia didn't answer.

Diana elbowed her husband. "Well, it took a while before lover boy here even noticed I was alive."

"That's not true," Marcel chimed in. "I noticed you. It's just that…you know, I…hell, who am I kidding? I was just an idiot. But luckily I came around."

"That's not so unusual," Louisa said. "Take me and my first husband, Robert. I was a dancer, and he was this magnificent horn player. Ooh, chile, he blew me away the first night I laid eyes on him. He was tall, dark, and, man, could he fill out a suit. But honey, I damn near had to club him over the head to get him to drop to one knee."

The men chuckled while Diana rolled her eyes.

"My point is," Lou said with a cocky grin, "that it's so easy to overlook something that's staring you right in the face."

Lou's and Ophelia's gazes met again.

"But I see you two are lucky."

Something about the woman's stare made Ophelia feel as if she was naked. And that, in turn, made her feel like a fraud.

"I love Jonas," she said defensively, as her grip on his hand tightened. "We're going to be very happy together."

Jonas puffed out his chest. "Sounds good to me."

Ophelia leaned in and extracted her own kiss from her willing fiancé. Desperately, she willed the sparks to come and the magic to flourish. It never happened, and she cursed her need for those stupid childhood fantasies.

Hours later, Jonas and Ophelia returned home. Jonas had to admit that he liked Marcel and Diana. He found their marriage to be an inspiration—not to mention, he loved the effect it was having on Ophelia.

Finally, they were back on track.

"I'm exhausted." Ophelia sighed, delivering a quick peck to his cheek. "I'm going to head off to bed."

Jonas quickly looped his arm around her and pulled her back. He nuzzled another kiss against the curve of her neck. "How about I keep you company tonight?"

Ophelia smiled. "We have an agreement."

He moaned in disappointment. "C'mon. It's been four months." He kissed her again. "I miss you."

She pulled away and chuckled softly. "It's just a few more weeks."

"Mmm. A lifetime. Why don't I grab a bottle of wine and put on some soft music?"

Ophelia squirmed farther away. "Sweetheart, you agreed."

"What's the matter—don't you miss me?"

"Of course I do, but I want to wait."

Jonas didn't want to quench the fire roaring through his veins, but her cool attitude was like a bucket of ice water. Once again, he felt the presence of another man. "Damn it, Ophelia. Don't do this."

She stiffened.

Jonas closed his eyes and finally dropped his arms to his sides. "Sorry," he said, without meeting her gaze.

For a few seconds they stood before each other in silence. Then, slowly, Ophelia reached out a hand and tilted his chin in her direction. When their eyes met, she surprised him with a question.

"Why do you love me?"

He blinked, thinking it was a preposterous question. "Because you're everything I've ever dreamed of," he said simply. "You're smart, kind, caring…and not to mention beautiful." He brushed his hand against the side of her face. "I look at you, I see everything I need to make me happy."

She stilled his hand and continued studying his gaze. After a while she pressed a tender kiss against his palm. "Good night," she whispered, and then turned and headed off to her bedroom.

When he heard the door close, it occurred to him that he had missed his opportunity to ask her the same question. Maybe that was a good thing.

Chapter 23

It took another two weeks before Jonas strolled through the offices of T & B Entertainment. His fiancée's demeanor had improved. She was laughing and smiling more, but it was the quiet times that disturbed him. As a wealthy man, he could give his future wife anything her heart desired. However, it was clear the one thing she wanted wasn't for sale.

Yet, Jonas wasn't a man without charm and persuasion—and he had a feeling he was going to need both of those things to pull this off.

He wasn't in the office long before he noticed the high traffic of beautiful women. Hell, he wouldn't mind working here himself.

"I'm here to see Mr. Bassett," he informed the young receptionist.

"Certainly." She smiled. "Do you have an appointment?"

He hesitated. "No. But I'm sure he'll speak with me. Can you tell him that Jonas Hinton is here to see him?"

"One moment." She punched a button on her keyboard and spoke to someone through her headset. She listened for a long time and even snuck a few questioning glances his way.

His antennae rose, and he had a sneaky suspicion he wouldn't get past the lobby. After deciding he should make his excuses and leave, the receptionist finally met his gaze.

"Mr. Bassett is in a meeting. You're more than welcome to have a seat in the lobby if you prefer to wait."

Jonas drew a deep breath, uncertain if this was a genuine offer or if he was being given the big heave-ho. But remembering he was there for Ophelia and not himself helped him make up his mind. "I'll wait," he stated, and then followed her directions to the small lobby.

After settling into a leather chair, he picked up the latest issue of *Vibe* and flipped through the pages. Several magazines later, his patience was reduced to a thin thread. A glance to his watch confirmed he'd been waiting well over an hour.

He stood and returned to the receptionist's desk. After another call, he was given the same line that Mr. Bassett was still in a meeting. He was tempted to leave, but he was determined not to give Solomon the satisfaction of getting rid of him.

Jonas returned to the lobby and started a new pile of magazines. Another hour slipped by, and his annoyance escalated.

Enough was enough.

As he stormed out of the lobby, he came within inches of smacking into Marcel.

"Oh, hey, man. What are you doing here?" Marcel asked, jabbing out his hand in greeting.

Jonas quickly slid on a smile and pumped his new friend's hand. "I came by to speak with Solomon, but it appears he's tied up today."

"Is he now?" Marcel nodded, his brows knitting together. "Well, let's go see what he's doing, shall we?"

The men breezed past the reception area, and Jonas's gaze occasionally drifted to one short skirt after another. A few of the women openly flirted with him, but since his heart belonged to another, it was easy to ignore all their signals.

"Afternoon, Chelsea," Marcel greeted. "Is Sol in?"

"Yes, sir." Her curious gaze shifted to Jonas, but she didn't stop them.

Jonas was impressed the moment he stepped into Solomon's spacious office. It appeared they had the same taste in décor and women.

"Hey, buddy," Marcel said. "What are you doing?"

Solomon turned from the window, but his gaze immediately narrowed on Jonas before shifting to his friend.

"It's good seeing you again, Mr. Bassett," Jonas said, squaring his shoulders. "I see you're finally out of your meeting. I hope I didn't catch you at a bad time."

Solomon boldly met his gaze. "I wasn't in a meeting."

The room immediately crackled with electricity.

"Well, I guess I'll leave you two alone," Marcel said with a lazy grin and turned back toward the door.

The look Solomon gave his friend as he retreated gave Jonas the distinct impression the man wished he could throw a few daggers at him. Once the door closed, Solomon's gaze shifted back to Jonas.

"What can I do for you, Mr. Hinton?"

Solomon left no room for dancing around the subject, so Jonas ditched the charm.

"I want you to talk to Ophelia." There, he said it, but it didn't mean his stomach didn't twist into knots. The last thing he expected was for Solomon to laugh at his request. "Did I say something funny?"

"You tell me."

Jonas felt challenged by his somber gaze, and he realized that this was harder than he imagined. "Look, I know you and Ophelia have a long history together. And I also know I'm responsible for what happened recently between you."

"Is that right?" Solomon moved away from the window and strolled over to the bar. "Want a drink?"

"Sure. Scotch on the rocks." Jonas remained off-kilter and confused by Solomon's reaction. He followed Solomon to the bar and then watched him as he prepared their drinks. Standing this close to him, Jonas noticed the tired lines etched around Solomon's eyes. They looked like the same ones around Ophelia's.

"So, what do you say, Solomon? Why don't we bury the proverbial hatchet and try to get along, for Ophelia's sake?"

"Can I be honest with you?" Solomon's dull gaze met Jonas's before setting his drink down in front of him.

Jonas shrugged. "Sure, why not?"

"I don't think that's a good idea."

Stunned, Jonas wasn't prepared for that answer either. For a few silent seconds, he watched Solomon take a few gulps of his drink.

"Mind if I ask why not?"

"Actually, I do mind." Solomon drained the rest of his drink, poured another, and then walked away.

"This thing is tearing Ophelia up inside. Surely you have to know that."

Solomon didn't answer. Instead, he made his way over to his desk and eased into his chair.

"Don't you care?"

"I care for Ophelia more than you'll ever know." Solomon's gaze lowered and he appeared thoughtful before he added, "But my answer is still no."

"You don't think this is just a little juvenile?"

"You mean like you forcing her to choose between us?" Solomon challenged, once again meeting his gaze.

"No. More like you trying to pay her back for not choosing you."

A spark lit in Solomon's eyes, but it quickly died. "There may be a little truth to that. But my answer is still no."

Frustrated, Jonas drew a deep breath and glanced around. For the first time, he noticed a few boxes packed in the corners. "Going somewhere?"

Solomon hesitated, and then answered, "I'm transferring to our New York offices. Atlanta has gotten a little too…crowded for me."

"Selma lives in New York, doesn't she?"

Solomon laughed. "She has nothing to do with this. Selma and I are just good friends—not lovers."

Jonas frowned, unsure if he should believe him. "Then why—?"

"Look, as much as I'm enjoying our reunion, I need to get back to work. You do remember your way out?"

"You're not making this easy."

"No, I'm not."

"So this is it? You're going to walk away from a twenty-five-year-old relationship?"

"Funny. That's the same thing I asked Ophelia."

Jonas tossed up his hands. "You're being a jerk."

"No, I'm doing you a favor," Solomon said.

Their gazes clashed again.

"You were right to worry about me," Solomon confessed coolly. "I don't just love Ophelia like a friend. I've been in love with her since I was eleven years old. I've been sitting on the sidelines waiting. That was my mistake. But burying the hatchet would require me to go back to sitting on the sidelines—and I just can't do that. Not anymore.

"My move to New York should make things easier— for everybody. I can get on with my life, and you two can get on with yours." Solomon winked at him. "Call it my little wedding present."

Jonas's grip tightened around his drink, but his heated gaze remained locked on his new enemy. "I guess I should thank you for your honesty."

"That's not necessary." Solomon lifted his glass in salute. "Just make sure you take good care of *our* girl."

Jonas drained his glass in a single gulp and then slowly set his glass down on the bar. "I'm out of here." He headed toward the door.

Solomon chuckled. "It was good seeing you. We should do it again some time."

"Don't count it." Jonas jerked opened the door and stormed out.

Chapter 24

Seven days before the wedding, Ophelia finally settled on a wedding dress. Actually, Kailua and Diana had selected it, but she was grateful it was one more decision out of the way. Standing in front of the mirror in the bridal shop's dressing room, she studied the intricate details of her strapless beaded white dress and marveled over how much she looked like a princess.

"Hey, come on out. We want to see you," Kailua yelled.

Ophelia drew a deep breath and slid on a smile before exiting the dressing room.

Kailua, Diana, and her mother all gasped when Ophelia stepped out from behind the curtain. Two of the store's female assistants helped her onto a small circular podium before she was transformed into a large pincushion.

"I just can't believe my baby is getting married," Ophelia's mother gushed with shimmering eyes.

"Don't start crying, Mom," Ophelia warned and wiped at her own tears. "See? It's contagious."

"How can we help it?" Diana said. "You look beautiful."

Kailua crossed her arms and bobbed her head. "Yeah, girl. I can't wait until Jonas sees you. You're going to knock his socks off."

"I hope so." Ophelia experienced a flutter of nervousness. In the back of her mind, she knew there was no sense in worrying. Jonas and her mother were on top of everything.

"Your father and I had dinner with the Hintons last night," Isabella said, approaching with the veil. "Interesting family."

Ophelia rolled her eyes, thinking of her first introduction to the former Broadway actress and the near-deaf real-estate tycoon. *Eccentric* was too mild a word to describe Jonas's parents—just like *spoiled* and *self-centered* did little justice in describing his two younger brothers, Sterling and Quentin. She was certainly lucky to have gotten the best one out of the bunch.

"Well, I, for one, am looking forward to meeting Jonas's brothers at the wedding." Kailua giggled. "Since Solomon isn't coming, then I'm just going to have to set my sights on the next millionaire available."

Diana and Isabella elbowed Kailua and gave her the evil eye.

Ophelia smiled at their efforts to avoid a taboo subject. "It's okay. You guys can stop trying not to mention Solomon. It's actually starting to get a little annoying." She chuckled.

Kailua smiled. "See? I told you she was over this

whole thing. It doesn't bother her in the least that Solomon is moving to New York on her wedding day."

"He's what?" Ophelia blinked, feeling momentarily off balance.

The elbows attacked Kailua again until she literally cried out, "What'd I do?"

Diana smiled and met Ophelia's questioning gaze. "We thought it was best not to tell you."

Everyone else avoided meeting her eyes. Ophelia winced yet again at another painful pinch in her chest, but she forced on a brave smile. Solomon really wasn't coming.

Until that moment, she didn't realize she'd harbored the hope of Solomon surprising her at the wedding. Hell, she was even pathetic enough to fantasize sharing a dance with him.

"Well, I'm sure his move to New York will at least make Selma happy."

Diana frowned. "Who?"

"Selma Parker. His girlfriend."

Laughter burst from Diana before she was able to cover her mouth with her hand. "Selma Parker...Solomon's girlfriend?" she asked, once she'd gotten a hold of herself. "I don't think so. Selma is happily married."

Ophelia held her head still while the crown of her veil was pinned in her hair. "I know she's married, but Solomon and Selma made it no secret that they were also a couple."

"Then they were pulling your leg," Diana insisted. "Solomon and Selma are really good friends, but I think you've been bamboozled."

"But why would he...?" Ophelia thought back to that day in his office, but then just dismissed it. "It doesn't matter. I tried to make amends and I invited him to the wedding. It's his loss if he doesn't come. I'm marrying Jonas Hinton and living happily ever after."

To take his mind off his pending nuptials, Jonas allowed his younger brothers, Sterling and Quentin, to drag him to their private box seats at the Georgia Dome to watch an Atlanta Falcons game.

Sterling, thirty and a near carbon copy of Jonas, except for two added inches of height, was a diehard bachelor obsessed with one thing: power. Throughout their childhood, Sterling worshipped the ground Jonas walked on; but as men, they often found themselves competing for the same corporate contracts.

Quentin, twenty-eight and the baby of the family, avoided hard work like the plague. After dropping out of Harvard, he'd spent the past seven years trying to find himself. However, everyone knew that Quentin could always be found at the hottest parties.

At first, Jonas thought it was a great idea to spend a Sunday with his brothers; but once he arrived, he realized he'd walked right into an old-fashion intervention.

"I'm just saying, I don't know why you have to marry the girl," Quentin said, handing Jonas a scotch on the rocks. "She's gorgeous, I'll hand you that, but definitely not worth giving up your freedom. No woman is."

Sterling chuckled. "You know, it's not too late to call the whole thing off. You can tuck her away in a nice penthouse somewhere with an allowance. That's better than marriage, if you ask me."

"That's why nobody asked you," Jonas joked.

"At least tell us you had her sign a prenuptial agreement."

"That—" Jonas's gaze sliced to his baby brother "—is none of your business."

"Oh, no," his brothers groaned, guessing the truth.

"Are you crazy, man?" Quentin sat up in his chair.

The crowd below cheered and rose to their feet.

"What happened?" Jonas's attention returned to the field to see if he could make out what he'd missed. He then looked to the television screen to see if there would be an instant replay.

Sterling reached for the remote and shut it off.

"Hey!"

"Hey, yourself," he responded. "Answer the question. Did you ask Ophelia to sign a prenuptial agreement?"

Jonas rolled his eyes and stretched his neck muscles. "There's no need."

Sterling placed a hand over his heart while Quentin looked as if he'd been struck dumb.

"Don't you two start. I already know what you're going to say, and I don't want to hear it."

"Do you also know we're going to have you committed?" Sterling asked. "No way are we going to allow you to marry some woman you barely know without a prenup. That's financial suicide."

"Say what you want. I'm not listening. Ophelia isn't a gold digger, and she has more class than all the women you two knuckleheads ever dated, combined."

"That's not saying much." Quentin shrugged. "Besides, class is highly overrated."

"Now, I'm going to have to agree with him," Sterling said.

Laughing, Jonas returned his attention to the field. "Look, I don't expect you two to understand. Just know I've made my decision, and I'm cool with it. Ophelia is everything a man would want. I feel lucky she's agreed to marry me."

"Hell, what woman wouldn't? I checked out that rock

on her finger. That had to set you back at least six figures," Sterling said.

"And it was worth every penny." Jonas winked.

"All right. It's your funeral."

"C'mon, guys," he said, managing to hold on to his sense of humor. "Is it going to kill you to just be happy for me? I love her and I'm willing to take a chance."

The doubting brothers paused to stare at each other and then fell back in their seats roaring heartily.

Jonas pretended to ignore them, but when their laughter refused to die, he couldn't stop his lips from curling. "You two are just playa haters."

"Oh, about that." Quentin slapped his back. "On your wedding day, we're going to have to confiscate your playa card. At least until after the honeymoon."

"Hell, after not getting any for five months, he may never come back from that honeymoon," Sterling added.

Quentin's eyes widened to the size of silver dollars. "What? Five months? You have to be kidding me."

Jonas reached over and popped Sterling on the back of the head. "That was between me and you, big mouth."

"You mean to tell me you and this chick haven't slept together in five months?" Quentin was still dumbstruck. "Why in hell did you agree to something like that?"

"Not that it's any of your business, but we wanted our wedding night to be special," Jonas said patiently.

"We?" Quentin barked, sloshing liquor over the bar. "What's this *we* crap? That sounds like a chick thing. And what's so special about it? Either way you go, it's going to be the first time you do it as man and wife. That's as special as it gets." Quentin turned up his glass.

"Unless she's a virgin," Sterling wondered aloud.

Quentin choked and spewed out his drink. "A what? What is that?"

"Do you two mind?" Jonas snapped. "You're talking about my future wife. It doesn't matter who said what or who agreed to what. This is just how it is, and I'm sorry I ever mentioned it." He popped Sterling again.

His brothers' silence lasted less than a second.

"So is she or is she not a virgin?" Sterling asked, chuckling.

"That is none of your business."

Sterling took his turn in smacking Jonas across the back. "Look, maybe I can sort of see why you might be tempted to go down this dangerous path. You're right. She's a beautiful woman. But bro, it's the beautiful ones you have to look out for."

"Yeah," Quentin intoned. "Don't you remember that song? The beautiful ones hurt you every time."

"You got it all twisted," Jonas insisted. "Ophelia is not like that."

"All right, bro." Sterling shrugged and finally gave up the fight. "I hope you're right...for your sake."

Chapter 25

"How often have you experienced this pain?" Dr. Woodward asked.

Solomon thought for a moment. "I really don't know," he said, frowning. "Maybe a few months. It sort of comes and goes." He held still while the doctor placed the cold stethoscope against his back.

"Breathe in for me."

Solomon followed the doctor's instructions. After a few more tests, the doctor jotted down some notes and rattled off more questions before he hit on one that gave Solomon pause. "Stress?"

"Well, I know a man in your line of work must deal with a lot of that, but has your workload increased—or maybe it's something in your home life?"

Hell there was nothing at home. There was no one waiting to see him. Maybe he should look into getting a pet.

"Mr. Bassett?"

"Uh, no. Everything is pretty normal," he lied. Since June, his whole world had been flipped upside down and turned inside out, but he would survive.

"What about your move?" Dr. Woodward asked. "When is that again?"

"Tomorrow," Solomon replied.

"Hmm." The doctor folded his arms and considered him. "Maybe—"

"No, no. That's not it."

"The only reason I asked is because you just had a complete physical in May, and all your results show you're in optimum health. But we can run them again if you like. I'll get Darla in here with the EKG machine. We can make sure nothing has snuck up on us."

Solomon agreed to the additional tests, and an hour later, he collected Selma from the waiting room.

"What did he say?" Selma asked, sliding her purse strap over her shoulder. She waited for his answer before budging.

"I'm fine. Just like I said," he told her, clasping her elbow in a firm grip.

She sighed and allowed him to lead her out of the doctor's office. Once they reached the elevator bay, she tugged his arm. "Maybe we should get a second opinion?"

He rolled his eyes and shook his head. "Let it go. It was just indigestion."

"Uh-huh." Selma folded her arms. "What exactly did you tell the doctor?"

Thankfully, the elevator arrived and Solomon wasted no time stepping into the small compartment.

Selma followed suit and kept her eyes glued on him. "Well?"

"Look, I appreciate the concern, Selma—"

"But?"

"But I'm more than capable of discussing chest pains with my doctor. Nothing showed up on the EKG or X-ray. Let's drop it."

"Fine," she snapped, and then allowed the small space to fill with silence.

The doors opened at the building's lobby, and the friends bolted out as if they were in dire need of air. The silence continued during their walk to Selma's rental car. However, the moment they settled into their seats both blurted out, "Sorry."

They glanced at each other with wobbly smiles.

Solomon took her hand. "Thanks for caring so much."

"Actually, I have an ulterior motive. I have to make sure you stick around long enough to take my boys to Disney World this spring." She started the car.

"Ah, the truth comes out." He chuckled.

"Hey, Marty and I took them once, and we're still recuperating. Of course, after you move to New York and are around my little monsters more often, you'll probably rethink this whole thing."

"Not on your life," he vowed. "I love children and can't wait to go."

"Spoken like a true single man."

Solomon held on to his smile and glanced out of his side window. Tomorrow was a big day. For him…and for Ophelia.

This time they fell into a comfortable silence during the rest of their ride, and for the first time in many weeks, he allowed his thoughts to drift to his former best friend. He remembered the last time he saw her just as vividly as the first. Regardless of what his future held or whom he would go on to love and marry, he doubted he would ever forget any memory of her. Despite all that had happened, he truly wished Ophelia the best love had to offer. She deserved nothing less.

Ophelia finally experienced her butterflies. However, it felt more like they were attacking her from the inside. It was just the wedding rehearsal, but she had serious reservations about whether her knees were strong enough to carry her down the aisle.

She glanced at her father—the Corporal, a tall man at six-foot-five, and just as much of an imposing figure at age sixty-nine as he was in his heyday in the military.

"Are you all right, baby girl?" he asked, undoubtedly noticing her fright.

Fleetingly, she thought about asking, no, begging him to find the quickest escape route; but in the next breath, she realized she was just being silly. "I'm fine," she whispered.

His gaze scrutinized her until he was satisfied. "You know," he whispered. "I think you've made a fine choice. This man seems to care for you very much."

She was shocked. Her father never said a kind word about anyone she'd dated. "Yes. Yes, he does," she answered.

The wedding planner breezed past and instructed everyone to take their places.

"Of course...never mind." He shrugged.

"What is it?"

"Nothing. It's not important."

Ophelia frowned. "Let me be the judge of that. What were you going to say?"

He met her gaze again. "Well, it's nothing against your, uh, fiancé. Like I said—he's a fine young man, but

I always thought you and that other young man would eventually hook up. Not that I prefer him or anything. I'm just…surprised."

There was no point in pretending she didn't know to whom he was referring, but she did manage to laugh at the notion. "His name is Solomon, Dad. And no, we were never going to hook up, as you put it. We were just friends."

The Corporal glanced around. "I know. I know. You've been telling me that for years. But I guess the way you two were always joined at the hip, I thought… Well, it doesn't matter. I was wrong, and you made an excellent choice."

She nodded and glanced away; but after a moment of thinking about it, she faced him again. "Does that mean if I had chosen Solomon, it wouldn't have been an excellent choice?"

He blinked. "No, no. Not at all. The other young man, er, Solomon, would have been a fine choice as well."

"Marcel?"

"Another good choice."

Smiling, she shook her head. "I take it you would've liked anyone I chose to marry."

"Like?" The Corporal laughed. "Now, I don't *like* any of them. No man is ever going to be good enough for you in my eyes, but I can respect your choice. And I can break the man's legs if he ever steps a toe out of line."

"Thanks, Daddy." She smiled sadly.

"What is it?"

"Nothing."

He kissed her forehead as the wedding march began. "Ready for a test run?"

"I am now."

* * *

Selma and Solomon arrived back at his place, where a team of movers were steadily packing, and occasionally breaking, his stuff. Fortunately, Selma thrived off being in charge and upon her return, she resumed bossing everyone around. However, there was one room Solomon insisted on packing himself: the music room.

He trusted no one else with his precious platinum plaques or his massive CD collection…and that included Selma. It also meant he would have some much-needed time alone. After an hour of the tedious chore, he took note of the time.

Eighteen hours to go.

How sad was it he had started counting down the hours? Shaking his head, Solomon once again told himself to embrace change. It was difficult, but he still hoped and yearned for love and marriage…and children.

Nothing was as hard as erasing the image of him doting on a little girl with long, sandy brown hair and golden-colored eyes. In some strange way, saying goodbye to his fictitious child was like being in mourning.

Drawing a deep breath, he returned to his packing. However, his gaze soon snagged on an old CD: Jodeci's *Forever My Lady.* A smile flittered at the corners of his lips, and for a brief moment, he actually imagined the scent of strawberries filling the room. Yet before he was whisked away by the old memory, he heard a light rap against the door.

He turned toward Selma's smiling face.

"You got a minute?"

"Sure." He returned the compact disc to its rightful place and gestured for her to enter.

"Not that I was snooping or anything—"

"I already don't like how this is starting off," Solomon said, folding his arms.

Selma held up a white envelope. "I found this in the kitchen."

The wedding invitation.

"I didn't know Ophelia mailed you a peace offering. Why aren't you going?"

Solomon opened his mouth.

"The truth," she added.

Solomon clamped his mouth shut and shook his head. He didn't want to have this discussion. Maybe it would've been better if he'd made a tape and just played it whenever people asked him the same question.

"You know," Selma continued, "it wasn't too long ago you told me you'd rather have Ophelia in your life as a friend than not at all. I mean, wasn't that the whole point of not pursuing a relationship? The friendship meant everything."

"Nobody likes having their own words thrown back at them," he joked to his unamused friend. "I was wrong," he said somberly. "I've been lying to myself. Is that what you want to hear? Well, there you go. I said it."

"You should go," she said, holding out the envelope.

"No."

Selma walked over to him and pressed the envelope into his hands. "Go. Tell her how you feel."

Solomon stared into her pleading eyes, and then lowered his gaze to the envelope.

"Go," she insisted. "Even if it's just to say goodbye."

Another Intermission

Chapter 26

Back at the Crown Room

"I think you're purposely drawing this story out to keep me on pins and needles," Toni complained. "When are we going to get to the wedding?" she gasped. "Wait. Was there even a wedding?"

The bartender approached. "Can I get you two anything else?"

"I'm good," she said.

Her handsome storyteller simply shook his head, and the bartender silently drifted away.

Toni glanced back at her companion with a million questions racing through her mind. His story had the makings of a daytime soap. Did Ophelia really love Solomon, or had the handsome, spontaneous Jonas stolen her heart?

"You know, I really don't know why I'm running

off at the mouth like this. My rehashing this story isn't going to change how things turned out."

Fearful she wouldn't hear the rest of the story, she carefully placed a hand against his arm. "Maybe not, but talking about things can be therapeutic."

His silence seemed to stretch for an eternity before he finally met her gaze. "I guess you want to hear the rest?"

Toni nodded and leaned in close.

"Let's see. Where was I?"

The Wedding

Chapter 27

The morning of November twelfth, Ophelia woke up in her suite at Château Élan to a soft rap at the door. She had a sneaky suspicion who was on the other side, and she was hesitant to open it. "Go away," she sang.

Jonas laughed. "C'mon. Open up. I just want to wish you a happy wedding day."

She peeled back the soft sheets and stood up from her bed. "I can't do that." She walked over to the door. "You know it's considered bad luck for the groom to see the bride before the wedding."

"I won't tell anybody," he coerced softly.

Smiling, Ophelia cracked opened the door and peeked out. On the other side stood her fiancé, holding a single long-stemmed rose.

He winked and flashed her a smile. "I brought this for you."

Her heart melted at the kind gesture, and she opened

the door farther to accept the thoughtful gift. When her hand reached out, he grasped it and brushed a feather-like kiss against her knuckles. "I'm looking forward to making you Mrs. Jonas Hinton."

"And I can't wait to become—"

"Hey, hey. What are you two doing?" Kailua's voice thundered from down the hall. "Get away from that door."

Before the engaged couple could react, Jonas was swept away by a group of Ophelia's closest friends.

"Bye, honey," Jonas called out. "I'll see you at the altar."

"It's a date," she shouted back.

The women switched gears and poured into Ophelia's suite to give her a verbal thrashing.

"I know. I know. I told him it was bad luck, but what can I say? I'm a sucker for roses." She shrugged and took a good whiff of her gift. Today was her day, and she was going to relish every moment of it.

The serving staff arrived and set up a breakfast buffet in her room for the women to nibble on while professional hair and makeup people gave everyone the glamour treatment.

The other single women all seemed to be smitten by the groom's handsome and rich brothers. However, Kailua made it clear she had set her sights on Sterling Hinton, and promised to do physical harm to any woman she found within ten feet of the guy.

Of course, that declaration was met with a hearty round of laughter.

Ophelia happily donned a pair of sweatpants and a T-shirt with the words *Mrs. Hinton* written across the top. The girls cheered and broke out into a chorus of "Going to the Chapel."

All in all, it was a wonderful morning, filled with fun and laughter. Ophelia tried to forget that only one thing, or rather one person, would be missing on her special day. But there was nothing she could do about it, and she was just going to have to accept it.

Jonas glanced at his watch. It was three hours to showtime, and he was a nervous wreck. Of course, his brothers weren't helping.

"Hey, I drove the Porsche," Quentin informed him, finally reaching for his suit. "We can still make a clean getaway."

"Will you knock it off?" Sterling said, finishing his breakfast. "Can't you see he's about to unravel?"

"Most men are, on that final walk toward the execution chair."

Sterling shook his head. "Just ignore him. Those who've never experienced love are often jealous of those who find it."

Jonas frowned. "Are you spitting sonnets now?"

"Nah. Mom says it all the time. Probably from some old play of hers." He sipped his coffee. "My point is, Quentin is jealous. He couldn't capture the heart of a quality woman if he tried."

"What?" Quentin thundered. "Are you tossing out a challenge, bro?"

"Don't be silly. I would challenge you to get a job first."

"Uncle." Quentin tossed up his hands. "Boy, you don't play fair, do you?"

"Not if I can help it."

Jonas cleared his throat. "Hello. Remember me? The nervous wreck?"

"You can't be a nervous wreck and not have a prenup. You need to be damn sure of this," Quentin said with uncharacteristic seriousness.

"Anyone ever tell you that you're like a broken record?"

"Yeah. You do—all the time."

"Well, add me to the list," Sterling said, standing and walking over to his big brother. "I, for one, am proud of you. This whole thing gives me hope that my special one might be out there, too. Though I'm not in a rush to meet her."

Jonas laughed, and it did a lot to calm him down. He glanced at his watch again. "You know, Ophelia should be downstairs taking pictures with her parents right about now. Can you do me a favor?"

"Sure. Just name it."

"Go take a peek and tell me how beautiful my bride looks. See if she looks happy."

Sterling laughed. "My. You really are nervous."

"If you can get her alone, tell her I love her."

"You got it, bro."

"Do you think Solomon is going to show up?" Diana whispered to her husband as they watched Ophelia and her mother pose.

"I wouldn't bank on it," Marcel said. "His flight to New York leaves shortly after Ophelia is supposed to say 'I do.'"

Diana nervously reached for his hand. "So, what do you think? Is she about to make a mistake, or is she truly in love with Jonas?"

Drawing a deep breath, Marcel thought about it, but ended up shaking his head. "I honestly don't know. Up until this summer, I thought I knew my two best friends pretty well, and I would have never thought things would have played out the way they have."

"Hey, Marcel," Ophelia called. "You're my maid of honor. Get your butt over here."

"That's best man of honor, thank you."

Diana rolled her eyes and pushed her husband forward. "Stop clowning around, and get in there." She crossed her arms when her gaze landed on a taller version of Jonas Hinton. "Hello," she said, wondering how long he'd been standing there. "I'm Diana."

"Nice to meet you." Coolly, he tilted his head and walked off.

"My money is on Solomon. No doubt he's going to show up and crash the party," Kailua gossiped to a group of women. "I mean, c'mon. Everybody knows how he feels about Ophelia, and I think she's just as crazy about him. She's just too stubborn to admit it."

"How could she not be in love with Jonas? He's rich and gorgeous," another bridesmaid said.

"Have you met or even seen Solomon?" Kailua asked. "Well, I have, and let me tell you, I've seen *all* of him. Solomon has my vote any day of the week."

"That good, huh?"

"Better. Ophelia hit the jackpot selecting him to pop her cherry."

The group of women gasped and gathered closer.

"Solomon was her first?" someone asked.

"Yeah, but you didn't hear it from me," Kailua continued. "And have you all noticed how she keeps calling Jonas the wrong name? I'm telling you, something's there, and if Solomon shows up today, we're in for an interesting wedding."

Sterling frowned and moved away from a concrete

column behind the bridesmaids. He was more than amazed at what he could find out in a large room full of women. But what the hell was he going to tell his brother?

A woman's laugh rang out, and Sterling turned to see Ophelia's mother tossing her arms around her daughter. He took a moment and watched the two women.

Ophelia was indeed breathtaking in her wedding gown. His heart leaped at the sight of her, but as he watched her, he noticed her smile wasn't as bright as the ones around her, and she seemed to keep glancing around, as if she was looking for someone.

Could it be this Solomon everyone was talking about?

He didn't know. Suddenly, he had a bad feeling about all of this. At long last, there was a break in activity with the photographer, and he warred with himself on whether he should seize the opportunity to deliver Jonas's message.

"Sterling."

Ophelia spotted him before he could make a decision. "Hey, beautiful," he said, approaching.

"What are you doing down here?" She smiled, walking over to him. "Don't tell me Jonas sent you down here to spy on me."

"Sounds like you know him pretty well."

"I am about to marry him."

He studied her and nodded. "He wanted me to deliver a message."

"And what's that?"

"He wanted me to tell you he loves you."

Ophelia's cheeks darkened prettily. "Well, tell Solomon I love him, too."

Sterling's smile froze.

"What?" she asked.

"Nothing. I better head on up. I think we're supposed to be getting ready to come down here when you guys are done."

She smiled and brushed a kiss against his cheek. "Now, don't you dare tell him what this dress looks like. It's supposed to be a surprise."

"You got it." As he watched her walk away, he drew in a deep breath. What the hell was going on? The long walk back to the elevators and his journey up to his brothers' floor took forever, and still ended too soon. Maybe in this case, silence was golden. After all, he'd only heard a bunch of gossip and a simple name switch. He's done that before. He knocked on his brothers' suite door and waited until someone opened it.

A nervous Jonas, completely dressed in his wedding attire, turned from the mirror to beam a smile at him, and Sterling's heart squeezed. "Hey, Quentin. Could you give me and Jonas a few minutes alone?" he asked.

Quentin's brows rose while his gaze shifted between the brothers.

Jonas nodded for Quentin to go ahead.

"All right. It's almost noon. Good enough excuse as any for a drink."

"One drink," Jonas warned. "You're not going to be drunk before the wedding starts."

Quentin saluted and strolled out the door.

Once they were alone, Jonas returned his attention to Sterling. "So what's up?"

Sterling stalled for a moment, slid his hands into his pockets, and then met Jonas's gaze. "What do you know about a guy named Solomon?"

Chapter 28

Solomon took a final walk through his empty house, certain he was going to miss the old place. He had traveled all around the world, but he had always considered Atlanta home. However, the city held way too many memories, and he would rather deal with them only during the occasional visit than every day.

He glanced at his watch. It was twelve-thirty. Two hours before his flight, but an hour before...

He cursed under his breath and wished he could just stop obsessing over this. Either he was going, or he wasn't. He slid his hands into his pockets and pulled out the crumpled wedding invitation. In the past twenty-four hours, he'd ripped it up, taped it back together, and balled it up, only to hand iron it back out.

Go. Even if it's just to say goodbye.

Solomon pushed Selma's words to the back his mind, but they kept coming back to haunt him, just like the memory of his one intimate encounter with his best friend. He remembered how he'd felt watching her sleep. He'd never felt so at peace before or since that moment.

He missed that feeling.

"Knock, knock."

Solomon turned and smiled wryly at his Uncle Willy. As usual, his uncle cleaned up well whenever he put on a suit. "Come on in, old man."

"Hey, I always say there are two things there's no cure for: old age and ugly—but money does one hell of a masking job for both."

Solomon shook his head as he approached him. "What are you doing here?"

"I came to see if you've come to your senses or, if not, I came to wish you bon voyage."

"Then thanks for coming to see me off. I take it you're going to the wedding?"

"What can I say? Ophelia personally invited me."

"And it's a good place to hit on some new women."

Willy winked and shot him with an imaginary gun. "You know me so well."

"Yeah. Lucky me."

The two men fell silent before Willy asked, "So, whatcha got there?"

Solomon crumpled up the invitation and slid it back into his pocket. "Nothing."

His uncle nodded, but his expression clearly reflected doubt. "Is there any way I can convince you you're making a mistake?"

"I can't watch her marry someone else." Solomon rubbed at the sudden pain in his chest.

"Then maybe she needs convincing she's marrying the wrong person."

Solomon laughed. "You keep surprising me with this hopeless romantic act you have going now."

"I'm nothing if not a bag of contradictions." He glanced at his watch. "Last chance. Are you sure you don't want to come?"

Solomon shook his head.

"Not even just to say goodbye?"

He stopped and stared at his uncle. It was the second time this was suggested to him. Maybe he should. Would it at least give him a sense of closure?

Willy slid an arm around his nephew's shoulders. "So, what do you say?"

It was twenty minutes before the ceremony, and Ophelia felt faint. Everyone scrambled around, getting her water and fanning her to cool her down. She kept saying she was fine, but in truth, she was feeling anything but. Who knew she could have so many conflicting thoughts crammed inside her head?

"Are you all right?" Diana asked, smiling.

Again she nodded. "Please tell me this is normal."

"Do you feel like you want to throw up?"

"Yeah."

"Perfectly normal," Diana assured with a wink.

Ophelia smiled, not quite sure if she believed her new friend. Every nerve in her body seemed to be twisted in knots, and the pain in her chest throbbed mercilessly. "You wouldn't happen to have some Tums with you?"

Diana blinked. "Uh, I can send someone to find some for you, if you like."

Ophelia lowered her head into the palms of her hands and combated another wave of nausea. "I think I'm going to need it. That, or some Pepto-Bismol."

"That bad?" Diana inquired.

"Why, is that not normal?" Ophelia asked with rising panic.

"Yes, yes. You're fine. I'll see if I can get Marcel to get you some." Diana sprang into action.

"Thanks, girls." Ophelia addressed her other bridesmaids. "You can stop fanning me now."

Everyone put down the numerous magazines and leaflets and glanced nervously at each other.

Ophelia suddenly felt like a freak in her own sideshow and didn't really know what to say to anyone. It appeared that they didn't have a clue either.

A quick knock came at the door, and Ophelia's mother rushed inside. "What's going on?" Her gaze found her daughter. "Someone said that you were sick. What's the matter?" She crossed the room and immediately placed her hand across Ophelia's forehead. "You're warm."

"Don't worry. I'm fine. You need to get out to your seat. Everything is going to get started soon."

"But—"

"Really, Mom. Please. It's all right."

"Okay." Isabella brushed a kiss against her cheek and then pulled out a silver box from her purse. "I can't leave until I give you this."

Ophelia's eyes lit up as she reached for the gift. "What—?"

"It's from your father and me. You need something new."

"Wait, wait." Kailua dashed across the room. "You'll need something old, and something blue."

Ophelia flashed her ring. "I have the blue covered." She opened the box and gasped at a pair of diamond teardrop earrings. "Mom."

Isabella leaned forward and planted another kiss

against her cheek. "We love you, baby. And we'll support whatever choice you make."

"Thanks, Mom." Ophelia smiled but wondered at her mother's meaning while she took out her diamond stud earrings and replaced them with her parents' gift.

"Well, I took the liberty of getting something old from your jewelry box this morning," Kailua announced and returned to Ophelia's side. "Maybe you'll remember this from years ago."

Curious, Ophelia opened the box and froze at the sight of her old tennis bracelet—Solomon's gift on her twenty-first birthday.

"Didn't you tell me this was a fake?" Kailua asked, withdrawing the bracelet and carefully loping it around Ophelia's wrist.

"Yeah. Solomon found a copy of the one I really wanted from this jewelry store. It's a convincing zirconium, don't you think?"

"A little too convincing—which is why I took it to be appraised. Honey, this little baby is real."

"What? But how? Solomon was broke in college."

"Maybe you should ask him." Kailua connected the prongs and smiled. "That's if you ever speak to him again."

Ophelia lowered her hand. The weight of her old bracelet seemed extraordinarily heavy—just like the engagement ring in the opposite hand.

Diana rushed back into the room with the wedding planner close on her heels.

"Believe it or not, we found you some Tums and some chewable Pepto-Bismol. Which ones do you want?"

"Give me two of each," Ophelia said.

Diana brows rose, but she obligingly unwrapped the tablets and placed them in Ophelia's hand.

The wedding planner clapped her hands to get everyone's attention. "I need you ladies downstairs. The carriages are ready."

The bridesmaids gathered excitedly and filed out of the room.

"Remember what I said." Isabella gave her a final kiss and rushed out of the room.

"Are you feeling any better?" Diana inquired.

In truth, the tablets seemed lodged in her throat, but Ophelia responded, "I'm doing much better. Thanks." She carefully stood up and took a last glance at herself in the mirror. To her, she looked like a deer caught in headlights. The weight of the jewelry on each hand increased, and the pain in her chest refused to ease.

"Are you ready, baby girl?" the Corporal asked from the doorway.

"As ready as I'll ever be," she whispered and turned a bright smile toward her father.

"Then let's get you married."

Framed against a landscape of lush vineyards and rolling hills in the northern reaches of Atlanta, the sixteenth-century style French Château Élan was the backdrop of Jonas and Ophelia's wedding. The crisp fall afternoon was perfect as six hundred friends and family members took their seats.

Yet despite the kiss of a cool breeze, Jonas felt stuffy and kept fingering his collar. When that didn't work, he worried about the fast pounding of his heart. Surely he wasn't about to have a heart attack.

The sound of carriages reached his ears, and in the next second the music changed and the processional music began.

Everyone turned in their seats to watch the first bridesmaid and groomsman walk down the aisle.

Jonas suddenly winced at a pain in his chest, and it was probably the first time his stomach ever twisted into knots. Of course, Quentin strolled down the aisle with his usual self-confident strut while silently flirting with the woman on his arm. Jonas rolled his eyes and waited patiently as the rest of the wedding party took their turn down the aisle.

The best man and man of honor strolled down the aisle without linking arms, but they still made an amusing sight. However, Jonas did his best not to meet Sterling's questioning gaze. When the men finally took their places, the music dramatically changed to the wedding march, and everyone stood and waited.

But after a few bars, the bride failed to appear, and people started glancing at one another.

Jonas closed his eyes and discreetly rubbed at the increasing pain in his chest. The march ended and after a brief pause, the organ player started again.

This time, Ophelia and her father stepped into view, and a collective sigh of relief rose just above the music.

Ophelia's beauty surpassed Jonas's expectations. As she approached, smiling, he was certain he'd forgotten how to breathe. What in the world had he done to deserve this woman? It was hard to believe he was just moments away from officially making her his wife.

When she at last reached his side, the Corporal leaned over and kissed his daughter's cheek.

All three turned to face the minister.

"Excuse me. Excuse me," a man's loud whispering reached Jonas's ear, and he glanced back to see a large man, toting a cigar, make his way to an empty chair.

Minister Bulmash smiled down at them before addressing the crowd. "We welcome you today to the marriage of Jonas William Hinton and Ophelia Rose Missler. We are met together in the presence of their dearest family and friends to join this man and this woman in holy matrimony. This is indeed a joyful time, in which we witness the love of these two people expressed in the joining of their lives together."

Jonas drew in a deep, steadying breath and glanced over at his bride, but before he was able to pull his gaze away, he noticed her hand fiddling with a bracelet on her arm, and then her ring. While the minister went on, he studied her face and noticed how she was growing paler by the second.

"Ophelia and Jonas, do you both come freely, and without reservation, desiring to commit yourselves to one another in this covenant of marriage?"

"We do," Jonas answered, and then waited for Ophelia to respond.

She swallowed and looked as if at any moment she was going to pass out. After another low rumbling of whispers, Ophelia answered in a small, pinched voice. "We do."

The minister smiled. "Who gives this woman to be married to this man?"

"Her mother and father," the Corporal announced, releasing his daughter's arm and stepping back.

The couple linked their arms together, the minister continued his sermon, and Jonas couldn't take his eyes off Ophelia.

"And now," the minister said with a rising voice, "if anyone knows any just cause why these two should not be lawfully joined together in matrimony, let them speak now or forever hold their peace."

"I object!"

Chapter 29

This time, when the gasp of surprise from the six-hundred-plus guests reached its highest decibel, one boisterous laugh rang out. "Ha! I knew it."

Ophelia and Jonas stared at each other, both stunned and relived they had objected at the same time. "I'm sorry," they said in unison.

"Excuse me," the minister whispered. "But what's going on?"

"Give us a few minutes," Jonas said, sliding an arm around Ophelia's waist and guiding her away from friends and family.

It took a couple of minutes to find a decent spot away from prying eyes and ears, yet they found one close to their tented reception room.

Again, both of them rushed out their apologies and tried to explain before both of them realized they shouldn't talk at the same time.

"You go first," Ophelia offered.

"No, you go," Jonas countered.

Immediately, Ophelia's eyes glossed with tears before she could get her trembling lips to open. "Oh God, I don't know where to being." When she finally got ahold of herself, she laid a hand gently against his soft face. "You're such a good man. I have no doubt that one day you'll make some lucky woman a wonderful husband."

The tears finally leaked from her eyes, and it seemed almost poetic how they seemed to match his.

Jonas calmly and gently removed her hand from his face and kissed the palm. "And I think you will make Solomon a very good wife."

For the first time in years, she couldn't get herself to protest or deny her feelings for Solomon. And boy, did she have feelings. She was suddenly drowning in them.

"I'm so sorry," she finally whispered. "I didn't know... I've been denying and ignoring the signs for so long that it's practically second nature. But standing there listening to Minister Bulmash, I suddenly knew. I just knew..."

Jonas nodded, but there was still a lot of pain etched across his face. "Yeah. I saw that," was his only response.

"Please say something. You can even yell if you want."

"I'm not going to yell. I'm just as guilty as you when it comes to ignoring signs or lying to myself," he confessed. "I wanted you so badly that I was willing to take you from the one you rightfully belong to. I knew Solomon was your match the moment I met him, and it's the only reason why I didn't like him."

"Jonas—"

"I'm going to be okay...eventually."

More tears slid from her eyes. "Are you sure?"

"No." He chuckled. "You're sort of a tough act to follow."

She felt worse.

"I may not like Solomon, but I think I understand him."

Ophelia frowned in confusion.

"I want you to be happy—even if it means it's with someone else."

Overwhelmed, Ophelia stepped forward and leaned up on her toes to press a kiss against his salty tears. When she lowered back onto her heels, she was surprised at how her engagement ring slipped easily off her finger. "This belongs to you," she said.

Jonas said nothing as she pressed the blue diamond into his hand.

"Your Ms. Right is still out there."

"Sure she is." He smiled and glanced at his watch. "You better get going if you're going to catch Solomon before his flight."

Ophelia nodded and gave him a final kiss. "Take care of yourself. Goodbye." She turned and raced back toward the astonished crowd.

Everyone turned in her direction, and a few were bold enough to ask what was going on, but Ophelia ignored them all as she searched for one man in particular: Uncle Willy.

"Where is he?" she asked, running up to him.

Willy responded with a lopsided grin. "Finally came to your senses, eh?"

Ophelia didn't have time for Willy's sarcastic commentary. "Willy, if you don't get up and take me to Solomon, I swear I'll make you eat that cigar."

"Ah, the lady wants a ride," he said, pushing his

meaty frame out of his chair. "Why didn't you just say so?"

"Wait, wait," Marcel yelled, catching up to them. "I think I can help."

One of the perks as vice president of a top record label was having a Hawker 800XP private jet at his disposal. But during the whole ride to the airstrip, Solomon kept second-guessing his decision not to go to Ophelia's wedding.

There was no point in seeking some kind of closure. Hell, he wasn't even sure what that meant. Saying goodbye and good luck wasn't going to make him feel any better. It was a silly notion.

Then why did he feel like he made yet another terrible mistake?

When it came to relationships, it was time for him to admit he was totally inept.

After pulling into the small airport, he parked in his reserved spot and was immediately greeted by a personal assistant.

"There's going to be a slight delay in takeoff, sir. The pilot and crew are still checking the plane."

Solomon frowned and inquired whether there was something wrong.

"I'm sure everything is fine, sir. We'll have you up in the air in no time."

He nodded and glanced at his watch as he headed toward the building. As soon as he walked into the building, the pilot greeted him and repeated the same excuse to him.

"Are you sure there's nothing wrong?" Solomon inquired again. Something about everyone's behavior set him on edge.

"No, sir. Everything is fine. We'll have you up in no time."

The near-verbatim repetition caused a crease in Solomon's brows, but he quickly dismissed the crew's odd behavior. He glanced at his watch again and realized with a sinking heart that Ophelia was now Mrs. Jonas Hinton.

"Is there anywhere I can get a drink around here?" he asked.

The End?

Chapter 30

Toni stared at the man beside her and then glanced out the glass doors toward the airplanes. "So, you're heading out?"

He nodded.

She hesitated and wondered if she should give the man her unsolicited opinion when it suddenly occurred to her that something wasn't right about his story. "Umm, I know I sort of coerced you into telling me your story and all—and it is one hell of a story—but how do you know that Ophelia didn't marry Jonas?"

Her handsome stranger glanced up at her with his brows furrowed.

"I mean," she went on. "If you're still here waiting for your flight, then how could you possibly know she didn't marry this guy?"

Finally he laughed and held out his hand. "We haven't been properly introduced. *I'm* Jonas Hinton."

Toni stared at him before she finally accepted his hand. "Then you're not...well, how did it all end?"

Jonas drew deep breath. "Well, from what I've been told..."

Stay...Forever

Chapter 31

"Mr. Bassett, you can board now," a young, perky stewardess tapped him on the shoulder.

"Thank you." He folded the newspaper that had barely held his attention and stood. "Is everything all right now?"

"Everything is perfect. Your bags have been loaded onto the plane."

He nodded and followed her out the small terminal's lobby. His plane had finally pulled out of its hangar and was waiting for him to board. As he headed toward the jet plane, Solomon gave the pilot at the foot of the stairs a playful salute. "I'm expecting a smooth flight," he joked nervously. Flying had never been his forte, and he had to admit he was more than a little concerned about their lengthy delay.

"I'm sure you'll enjoy your trip."

He held his smile, climbed the stairs, and entered the luxurious cabin.

"Hello, Sol."

Solomon's head jerked toward the familiar voice, but he most certainly didn't believe his eyes. She looked like an angel in her stunning white gown and with hope and tears shining in her eyes. "What—?"

"I hope you don't mind me delaying your flight," she said in a shaky voice. "But it was important I talk to you…and since you're not exactly returning my calls, I figured I could capture your attention this way."

"You succeeded," he said, but in the next second he shook his head. "Aren't you supposed be getting married right now?"

A nervous laugh escaped her as she rolled her eyes. "Well, there's a slight problem with that."

He frowned. "What sort of problem?"

Her golden eyes locked with his as she drew a deep breath. "The problem of me being in love with you."

Solomon stared at her, unable to blink, let alone breathe.

"Now, I know this may come as a surprise to you," she said, stepping forward, "seeing how I've never told you or let on about how I felt." She paused for a nervous laugh. "But there's a reason for that."

"Which is?" he asked out of reflex.

"I didn't know until today…or maybe I knew but was too scared to risk losing you forever."

"But then you shut me out—"

"And it was like tearing out my heart—and that was exactly what I did. Whenever your name came up or I thought about you, I would get this horrible pain in my chest. I tried to blame it on everything but the truth."

She stopped within inches of him. "Please tell me I haven't lost you."

Solomon closed his eyes and then immediately felt her hand against his face. He captured it, kissed it, and then placed it over his heart. "It seems we've been having the same pain."

He finally opened his eyes and gazed into a face radiant with love. He leaned forward and kissed the soft petals of her lips. That was all it took to send his heart soaring. His arms wrapped around her waist, and he pulled her against him. And still he couldn't believe she was actually there—in his arms and saying the words he had waited twenty-five years to hear.

"You haven't lost me," he said, breaking their kiss. "I loved you since the day we played ten minutes in heaven. For some reason I could tell everyone but you how I felt. Sometimes that one night we spent together seems more like a fantasy than any real thing I know. I desperately wanted you to wake up that morning and be in love with me."

"Silly charts and statistics. More excuses not to take a chance. Don't move to New York. Stay…stay here with me forever."

"Correct me if I'm wrong, but that sounds strangely like a proposal."

Her voluptuous lips widened while her eyes twinkled at him. "And what if it is?"

Solomon leaned down for another tantalizing kiss. "Then I accept."

"You just made me the happiest women in the world." She leaned up on her toes and kissed him again. "Do you think we can get the pilot to take us to Las Vegas?"

"Vegas?"

"Well, I'm already dressed for a wedding."

Smiling, Solomon stole another kiss. "In that case, Vegas, here we come."

Chapter 32

The strangest things always seem to happen in Las Vegas. The infamous city always had a way of freeing people of their inhibitions. Visitors fall in love with complete strangers somewhere between the hours of two and three a.m.

However, that wasn't the case for longtime best friends Ophelia and Solomon. After so many years, the couple had finally realized that everything they had ever wanted was in each other.

Upon landing, a limousine whisked them away to Clark County Marriage Bureau to obtain a license. Their next stop was to the Little White Wedding Chapel.

To Solomon's great relief, an Elvis impersonator did not perform the honors, but two newly married eighteen-year-olds signed as witnesses to the union of Ophelia Rose Missler and Solomon Elijah Bassett.

An hour later, Solomon carried his bride across the

marble entry of their MGM Grand Penthouse suite. "Here we are, Mrs. Bassett," he said, accepting her lips in yet another kiss.

"Have I told you how much I like the sound of my new name?"

"At least a hundred times, but you know me. If you like it, I love it." He kicked the door shut.

"You know what I would love right about now?"

"I'm hoping it's the same thing I'm thinking of." He chuckled, carrying her upstairs to the bedroom.

"Ooh, you know what? Maybe we should call for some strawberries and whipped cream," she joked. "I seem to remember we never got to those the last time."

"Sounds good to me."

At long last, he arrived at the bedroom and lowered her onto her feet. "Did I tell you how beautiful you look in this dress?"

"I'm glad because it's the only thing I have to wear." She laughed and then just stared at him. "We did it."

"Yeah." He lifted her hand and pressed a kiss against the fifty-dollar ring he'd purchased at the chapel. "I want you to know I'm going to replace this as soon as we get back to Atlanta."

"Don't you dare." She snatched back her hand. "I love this ring. It's not too heavy."

Solomon frowned. "What?"

"It's a long story."

"Okay." He leaned down and began nibbling on her earlobe.

She moaned and melted against him. It wasn't long before their lips melded together and elevated the newlyweds to wondrous heights.

Solomon's large hands worked their magic on her dress buttons and zipper. In seconds, the heavy material dropped and pooled around his wife's feet. He quickly discovered the dress was nothing compared to her lacy bra, panties, thigh-high stockings, and garter belt.

"Good Lord," he whispered.

Ophelia chuckled and slid him out of his shirt. "I think you need to catch up."

Once she had him down to just his boxers, her husband swept her back into his arms and gently placed her down on the bed. As his mouth returned to hers, his hands roamed over her body.

Solomon swallowed her low moan and found the bra's hook in the front. He pulled his lips away long enough to watch the unveiling of her full, lush breasts. His memory had done them little justice, but their sweet taste was just as he remembered.

Sighing, Ophelia arched her back and aided in filling his hot mouth while her hands roamed freely along his short-cropped hair. During his pleasurable suckling and sporadic nibbling, she found it impossible to control her squirming.

However, Solomon was in no rush, and he teased her mercilessly by roaming his hands over every inch of her body before finally unsnapping the hooks to her garter belt and pulling off her delicate panties.

In a bold and surprising move, Ophelia rolled her husband over and onto his back, and then smiled as she took the dominant position. "You know, I owe you a favor," she said, tugging down his boxers.

"Oh?" he asked with a half grin.

"Uh-huh." She leaned forward and started raining tiny kisses along his broad chest and down his tight abs. His arousal continued to harden until it throbbed. The sight of her lips closing around his straining flesh was nearly enough for him to explode, and so was the feel of the slick walls of her hot mouth. His self-control held, but he knew if he didn't take her soon all bets were off.

Ophelia laughed when he lifted and pinned her beneath him almost in the same motion. She braced herself and wasn't disappointed at how her husband eased into her and filled her completely. Within a few strokes, his name drifted from her lips like a soft song—a song that was in perfect harmony with her heart.

Her response to him was like an erotic Picasso to Solomon. There was nothing more beautiful than to watch her in the throes of passion and to feel her squeezing every inch of his shaft. Heaven included the feel of her silky legs wrapped around his hips and the feel of her nails kneading his back.

Tears leaked from Ophelia's eyes at the beauty of their lovemaking. She hadn't realized how much she'd missed his lips, touch, and body. Now, she couldn't seem to get enough of him. The thought of being able to hold him like this for the rest of their lives moved her like nothing else.

She loved this man and wanted to scream her declaration from every rooftop in Vegas. Her best friend was now her lifelong companion—just as it should be.

As time ticked on, their bodies rocked in the sexiest tempo until her wet heat sent several shudders of pleasure rippling through him. When a thin film of sweat covered their bodies, Ophelia's inner walls tightened with her first explosion.

Solomon stilled his movements, grimacing through the sweet torture. "How do you feel, baby?" he asked, while he waited for her to relax again.

Her answer was in another kiss. It was amazing how her lips grew sweeter each time he tasted them. He moved inside of her once again and managed to fool himself that he was in complete control as long as he continued with long, measured strokes.

Minutes later, he knew he was in trouble when his breathing became choppy and a fire lit within him. Soon his thrusts became hard and fast. He didn't want the ecstasy to end, and he sank deeper into her. His jaws clenched at the feel of her tightening again. She cried out his name, and he growled his release.

Sated, Solomon rolled to his side and drew her pliant body against him. Waiting for their labored breathing to return to normal, Solomon peppered kisses against her head while she planted a few along his chest.

"Do you think it will always be this good between us?" Ophelia asked, sighing and nuzzling closer.

"We have a good shot as long as you don't bring up any more charts and statistics."

"You know, you could've come clean at any time, too, lover boy."

"Yeah, I know." He squeezed her tighter. "Let's promise that from now on, we're completely honest with each other."

"Sounds good. Why don't we start with you telling me how you were able to afford this real diamond tennis bracelet back when you were a poor college student?" She held up her wrist.

He smiled. "I thought we agreed that the price doesn't matter. It was the thought that counts."

"Yeah, but—"

"Well, let's just say I thought very highly of you."

Ophelia dropped her hand and lifted her head to stare up at him while she waited for a real answer.

"Fine. I borrowed the money from Marcel's dad. I've long since paid him back."

"How did I miss so many clues?"

"Does it matter now? We're together—forever."

"Forever," she whispered. "I like the sound of that."

"If you like it—" Solomon leaned in for a kiss "—then I love it."

Epilogue

"Flight 1269 to Los Angeles is now ready for boarding."

"Oh, that's me." Toni dabbed her eyes and then slid her purse strap over her shoulder before she glanced at Jonas again. She didn't quite know what to say to such a bittersweet love story, especially since he had gotten the short end of the stick. "It looks like I did a lousy job in cheering you up," she admitted.

Jonas's adorable dimples flashed. "I don't know about that. It felt good to finally talk about it. It's been a year, and Lord knows, my brothers, though well intentioned, have been unsuccessful in getting me to open up." He met her gaze. "Looks like you are a good listener."

"A year, huh?" Toni's interest perked.

"Yeah. I heard Ophelia and Solomon had a beautiful girl last month. For the most part, I've been able to move on. I'm a little nostalgic because today would've been our one-year anniversary."

Toni nodded as she studied him. "You know, I bet she was right about you," she said. "One day, you'll make some woman a wonderful husband."

Jonas leaned back and crossed his arms while he studied her for the first time. "Is that right?"

A delicious warmth swept throughout Toni's body, and if she was standing, she was certain her knees would've buckled.

"Now boarding flight 1269 to Los Angeles..."

Reluctantly, Toni stood from her bar stool. Where Ophelia and Solomon were fearful in taking a risk, Toni certainly was not. Quickly, she reached into her purse and withdrew a business card. "If you're ever in Los Angeles, give me a call."

Still watching her, Jonas accepted the card. "I just might do that, Ms...." He glanced at her name and a wide smile eased across his lips. "Ms. Wright."

"Until then." She winked, and then made sure she swished her hips in just the right way as she strolled out of the Crown Room.

Jonas enjoyed the view as he pocketed the card. "Until then, Ms. Wright."

* * * * *

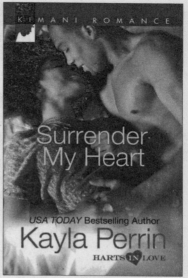

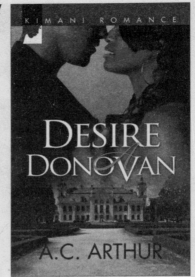

For lovers only…

Everything to ME

KIMANI ROMANCE

SIMONA TAYLOR

When Dakota Merrick jets down to the Caribbean, she doesn't expect to spend the night with Trent Walker. But Dakota's enchanted by the passionate music she and Trent make together. Then a breaking scandal threatens their tropical idyll. Will Dakota choose ambition over passion? Or can Trent find the right notes to play a love riff straight into her heart?

"Taylor has a superb flair for developing drama and romance."
—*RT Book Reviews* on *Love Me All the Way*

KIMANI **HOTTIES**
It's All About Our Men

Available June 2012
wherever books are sold.

KIMANI™
ROMANCE

www.kimanipress.com

REQUEST YOUR FREE BOOKS!

2 FREE NOVELS
PLUS 2 FREE GIFTS!

KIMANI™
ROMANCE

Love's ultimate destination!

YES! Please send me 2 FREE Kimani™ Romance novels and my 2 FREE gifts (gifts are worth about $10). After receiving them, if I don't wish to receive any more books, I can return the shipping statement marked "cancel." If I don't cancel, I will receive 4 brand-new novels every month and be billed just $4.94 per book in the U.S. or $5.49 per book in Canada. That's a saving of at least 21% off the cover price. It's quite a bargain! Shipping and handling is just 50¢ per book in the U.S. and 75¢ per book in Canada.* I understand that accepting the 2 free books and gifts places me under no obligation to buy anything. I can always return a shipment and cancel at any time. Even if I never buy another book, the two free books and gifts are mine to keep forever.

168/368 XDN FEJR

Name   (PLEASE PRINT)

Address   Apt. #

City   State/Prov.   Zip/Postal Code

Signature (if under 18, a parent or guardian must sign)

Mail to the **Reader Service:**
IN U.S.A.: P.O. Box 1867, Buffalo, NY 14240-1867
IN CANADA: P.O. Box 609, Fort Erie, Ontario L2A 5X3

Not valid for current subscribers to Kimani Romance books.

Want to try two free books from another line?
Call 1-800-873-8635 or visit www.ReaderService.com.

* Terms and prices subject to change without notice. Prices do not include applicable taxes. Sales tax applicable in N.Y. Canadian residents will be charged applicable taxes. Offer not valid in Quebec. This offer is limited to one order per household. All orders subject to credit approval. Credit or debit balances in a customer's account(s) may be offset by any other outstanding balance owed by or to the customer. Please allow 4 to 6 weeks for delivery. Offer available while quantities last.

Your Privacy—The Reader Service is committed to protecting your privacy. Our Privacy Policy is available online at www.ReaderService.com or upon request from the Reader Service.

We make a portion of our mailing list available to reputable third parties that offer products we believe may interest you. If you prefer that we not exchange your name with third parties, or if you wish to clarify or modify your communication preferences, please visit us at www.ReaderService.com/consumerchoice or write to us at Reader Service Preference Service, P.O. Box 9062, Buffalo, NY 14269. Include your complete name and address.

KROM11B

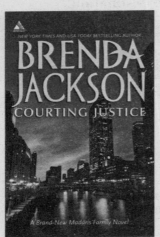